James Pattinson is a full-time author who, despite having travelled throughout the world, still lives in the remote village where he grew up. He has written magazine articles, short stories and radio features as well as numerous novels.

CRANE

Paul Crane had not altogether liked the look of Skene and West when they turned up at his north Norfolk cottage and made him an offer he could not refuse, but his chequered past had taught him not to be particular. Down on his luck since eighteen, when he was picked up on Liverpool Street Station by the decidedly odd Heathcliff, Crane promptly teamed up with a young thief named Charlie Green. Only when he fell in love with Penelope was there any hope of going straight. And perhaps he would have stuck to his promise if the chance of making a million had not dropped into his lap.

JAMES PATTINSON

◆

CRANE

Complete and Unabridged

ULVERSCROFT
Leicester

First published in Great Britain in 2001 by
Robert Hale Limited
London

First Large Print Edition
published 2002
by arrangement with
Robert Hale Limited
London

British Library CIP Data

Pattinson, James
    Crane.—Large print ed.—
    Ulverscroft large print series: adventure & suspense
    1. Suspense fiction
    2. Large type books
    I. Title
    823.9′14 [F]

    ISBN 0–7089–4764–6

Published by
F. A. Thorpe (Publishing)
Anstey, Leicestershire

Set by Words & Graphics Ltd.
Anstey, Leicestershire
Printed and bound in Great Britain by
T. J. International Ltd., Padstow, Cornwall

This book is printed on acid-free paper

1

Two Men In Suits

Crane was leaning on the gate at the front of his cottage when the men drove up. There were two of them and he did not care for the look of either. They looked like trouble to him.

The car was a Mercedes-Benz; black, fairly new, giving an impression of opulence. Own a car like that and it was likely you had money; plenty of it.

The one sitting in the passenger seat lowered the window and said: 'We're looking for a guy named Crane. Paul Crane. You know where we can find him?'

He was a hard-faced character with a scar on the left-hand side of his nose. Maybe some ill-disposed person had tried to slice it off a while ago and had made a botched job of it. It had done nothing to improve his appearance. One would hardly have expected it to.

'I know,' Crane said.

'So?'

'So what?'

'So are you going to tell us?'

'You have any good reason why I should?'

The second man, the one behind the wheel, gave a laugh. It was like the bark of a dog, sudden and brief. He was heavy-featured, the skin of his cheeks pitted, as though by a scattering of shot from a four-ten gun.

'You wouldn't be the man himself by any chance?' He had a gravelly kind of voice and he wheezed slightly. Possibly he smoked too many cigarettes. His hair was cropped close to his scalp, but you could see that he had been losing it anyway. He was maybe in his early forties.

'Why wouldn't I?' Crane said.

'Look,' the first man said. 'Let's not play games. My name's Skene, Joe Skene, and this is Sam West. We'd like to have a talk with you.'

'About what?'

'Business.'

'I'm not in business,' Crane said. 'I've retired.'

Which was not strictly true.

'Like hell you have!' the man with the scar said. He was evidently of the disbelieving kind.

And then they were both getting out of the car and coming up to the gate, leaving the

Merc parked in the lane. They were wearing dark suits and highly polished black shoes, which made them look somewhat out of place in that neck of the woods. People around there tended to be more casual in their dress. Crane himself was wearing brogues and jeans and an open-necked check shirt. He had a lean, suntanned face and hair that looked as though it had been bleached. He was around five-ten in height and eleven stone in weight and there was no excess fat on him worth mentioning. He was thirty-five years of age and sometimes felt older. Especially now that Penny had gone. Losing her was enough to make any man feel old.

When they reached the gate the men came to a halt. Crane stood on the other side, just looking at them and making no move to open it.

'You going to let us in?' Skene asked.

'Now why would I do that?' Crane asked.

'Might be better to talk inside.'

'If there's anything to talk about.'

'Oh, there is. Believe you me.'

Crane decided it might be as well to let the men come in. They did not look like the sort who would be easily turned away. They had maybe travelled some considerable distance to see him, possibly from as far away as London. They spoke like Londoners — the

3

East End kind — though the Mercedes car and the obviously expensive clothes indicated a certain affluence; as did the gold watch that could have been a Rolex on Skene's wrist. West had some gold accessories too: a ring in the lobe of each ear and a chain round his neck. There was also a tattoo on the back of his left hand. It was the representation of the head of a snake, the forked tongue darting out and the body of the reptile disappearing under the cuff of his jacket. How far up the arm it stretched could only be guessed.

'Okay then,' Crane said, 'if you say so.'

He lifted the latch of the gate and pulled it open.

The fact was that his curiosity had been aroused and he wanted to know just what it was that had induced the two men to pay him this visit. There had never been any real likelihood of his turning them away without a hearing.

There was a shingle path leading up to the front door of the cottage, which was an old flint building with a slated roof. It stood on rising ground, which saved it from flooding on those occasions when abnormally high tides brought the North Sea raging over the marshes. From the front windows you could see the channel which meandered through them, finally to join that greater expanse of water across which in former times had come the feared marauders from Scandinavia and The Netherlands.

Crane led the way up the path, the two visitors following close at his heels. He opened the front door and ushered them inside. There was no entrance hall; you walked straight into the living-room. There was a motley collection of furniture which looked as though it might have been picked up secondhand here and there at auction sales and junk shops, no two pieces matching. A worn carpet covered part of the floor, and there was a fireplace with some dead ashes lying in a heap on the hearth. On the mantelpiece was an old clock ticking away and a lot of cheap bric-a-brac. At the back of the clock were some envelopes that might have contained bills.

'Living in the lap of luxury, I see,' West said.

Crane made no reply to the jibe, but it had touched a nerve. The cottage had been one of the reasons why Penny had left. She had said she could no longer put up with living in squalor: that was her word for it. Which was rather an exaggeration, he thought. Certainly the place was a bit rough, even a bit primitive, but surely not squalid.

And of course she had loved it at first. It

was so nice, she said, to get away from the rush and bustle of London; away from the stress of living in the metropolis. Stress, she said, was the bane of city life; it was what drove people to drink and drugs and maybe to the overdose which would end it all. None of which of course had stopped her from flying back to it when the more primitive way of life had become just too much for her.

Everything had been fine at first; roughing it a bit was nothing to worry about. And besides, she could always nip up to London in her Mini if something came along, like a small part in one of the TV soaps or an advertising slot maybe. There was no telephone in the cottage, but she had her mobile and her agent could get in touch with her at a moment's notice if he had anything for her. Which, to tell the truth, did not occur with any great frequency.

But she had gone, and her going had left a gap in his life.

2

Penny

It was in a TV advertisement that he had first seen her. She was sitting on the bonnet of a car wearing nothing much at all: just a fairly skimpy bikini that hid few of her charms. And there were plenty of these, to his way of thinking.

He was hooked straightaway. He had to get to know her. He could never remember afterwards what was being advertised; maybe it was the car, maybe something else. All he remembered was the girl; a brunette with gorgeous eyes and an enchanting smile.

Not that there was much of a smile on her face when he finally got to see her after making all sorts of enquiries here and there. She was not in a good mood. She told him later that he had caught her at a really bad time. She had just missed out at an audition for a small part in a new West End production and was ready to kill somebody, anybody. And then he turned up; a complete stranger with some crazy suggestion that maybe she would like to have dinner with him.

'Why in hell,' she said, 'would I want to do that? I don't even know you.'

'Well,' he said, 'we can soon put that right. I'm Paul Crane. And you, of course, are Penelope Winter. I saw this ad on TV. You were in it, sitting on the bonnet of a car.'

'Oh that!' She frowned and he got the impression that she was not at all pleased to be reminded of it. 'You have to take what comes. Beggars can't be choosers.'

'I had to find you. I came up to London just to do that.'

'You're kidding,' she said.

He denied the suggestion. 'It's the truth.'

'So you're not a Londoner?'

'Not at present, no. I've got a place in North Norfolk. On the coast.'

He thought it best not to tell her what kind of place it was. He doubted whether she would have been impressed. And above all he wished to make a good impression.

She stared at him. 'But that's crazy. You know nothing about me. You don't even know whether or not I'm married.'

'Are you?'

'No, but — '

'So now I know. And before you ask, I'm not either.'

'I wasn't going to ask.'

'So how about it?'

'About what?'

'Dinner with me.'

'But it's only four o'clock, for God's sake.'

'Is it? Well, how about afternoon tea? For starters.'

He thought she was going to refuse, but after some hesitation she gave a sigh and said: 'All right then. I must be crazy too, but OK. I can use some refreshment. And you'll be paying, I hope.'

'Of course.'

★　★　★

And that was the start of it. The rest followed on from there. It turned out that she was sharing a pretty seedy flat with two other Thespian hopefuls. It seemed there were still far too many Mrs Worthingtons ignoring Noël Coward's advice and putting their daughters on the stage. Or at least trying to. Though perhaps it was not really the mothers who were to blame but the daughters themselves, dazzled by the glamour of the boards and the footlights, only to find that the hard reality was far different from what they had imagined. There was not much glamour attached to standing in a queue waiting for an audition with a hundred other applicants and then failing to get the part. As Penelope explained to him, it was all so galling when you knew you had talent. And of course if you were not convinced of that, what hope was there?

She herself was not without qualifications; there was no doubt about that. She had been a RADA student; which was to say that she had studied acting at the Royal Academy of Dramatic Art. And she had not been one of the worst of graduates; in fact she had done rather well. Which made it all the more depressing to be driven to accepting such jobs as sitting in a bikini on the bonnet of a car for advertising purposes. It was not the kind of thing she had had in mind when setting out on a theatrical career.

'It's so damned degrading,' she said, when opening her heart to Crane on one occasion after their first meeting. 'Advertising a bloody car. A Japanese one at that.'

He wondered whether she would have felt less degraded if the car had been British. A Rolls-Royce perhaps. But was even a Rolls truly British these days? Anyway, he was glad she had taken the job. He might never have found her otherwise.

★　★　★

She came from a respectable home counties family. Her father was a successful estate agent with a large house that he himself would probably have priced at maybe a quarter of a million if it had ever come on to the market. Not that it was at all likely to in the near future. Arnold Winter was perfectly content to live where he did, and Mrs Winter had no hankering for anything more grand. Besides which, there was that villa in Spain to which they could always retreat when they felt the need for a change of scene.

Penny had had an expensive education at a select girls' boarding school, and the idea of her going on the stage had never entered either parent's head until she put it there. Mary Winter was no Mrs Worthington and did her utmost to dissuade her daughter from doing anything so rash when there were any number of less risky careers open to her. Arnold Winter was more neutral. If that was what the girl wanted he was not going to stand in her way. He guessed it would cost him money, but he had plenty. Her brother Peter, younger than she and destined to go into the family business, thought it might be fun to have an actress sister; especially if she became famous; as he had no doubt she would.

But the going had been tough. She

discovered that in the acting profession you were lucky if you did not spend much of the time resting. Which was a euphemism for being out of work. So you did other jobs simply to keep the wolf from the door while you waited for the big break to come along. She could always have relieved the financial situation by putting the bite on her father; he would have stumped up readily enough. But she hesitated to do that except as a last resort because it would have looked too much like an admission of failure.

'Some day,' she told Crane, 'I'm going to make it. I know I am. It may take a bit more time but I'll get there in the end.'

He wondered whether she was just kidding herself, but he did not suggest it. And maybe she was right. He knew nothing about her acting ability, though he could see that she had the beauty; anyone could. But this was not everything you needed in her profession; there were plenty of attractive young women with stunning figures going the rounds, but only a tiny minority of these would make it to the top.

He did not mention this to her. He just said: 'I'm sure you will. We'll see your name up in lights and it'll be great. I'll cheer like mad.'

She looked pleased and gave him a hug for

that; but he did wonder how long it would be before she gave him the push if she ever did make the grade to the big time.

He was reticent about his own background at first, though he did tell her that his parents were dead, killed in a road accident. He had been six years old at the time, an only child, and had been somewhat reluctantly adopted by an uncle and aunt who had two children of their own and never ceased to tell him how lucky he was to have been taken in hand by them and how grateful he ought to be for all they were doing for him. He felt neither lucky nor grateful. He knew they had no love for him and he felt under no obligation to love them in return. He disliked his cousins too; a feeling which was reciprocated by them.

Things might have been all so different if his mother and father had lived. He might never have gone to prison.

★ ★ ★

That was one of the episodes in his life which he did not mention to Penny at first. It was hardly the kind of thing that seemed likely to count in his favour, and he was very keen to present himself to her in the best possible light.

Yet, when he did eventually tell her, he was

13

amazed to discover how calmly she took the revelation. It did not appear to shock her at all. But by that time they had been lovers for quite a while and were living together in the cottage on the North Norfolk coast.

3

An Offer

'You going to give us some refreshment arter we've come all this way to see you?' Skene asked.

Crane stared at him with distaste. 'Why should I? I didn't invite you here and I feel under no obligation to play the genial welcoming host.'

West gave a laugh. 'I don't think he likes us, Joe. I really don't.'

'I neither like nor dislike you,' Crane said. 'I'm impartial. I know nothing about you. I never saw you before in my life.'

'That's true,' Skene said. 'You gotta admit, Sam, the guy has a point there. All the same, Mr Crane, I reckon you're likely to see quite a bit more of the two of us in the near future.'

'Is that a fact?' Crane said. 'Well, I wouldn't bet on it.'

'I would,' Skene said. 'And now how about a spot of the old refreshment? I really got a thirst on me, and I never did like discussing business with a dry throat.'

Crane hesitated, half inclined to refuse

15

point-blank to provide any kind of hospitality for these two unwanted guests. But he could see that he was not going to get rid of them in a hurry, since they had obviously come with a purpose and would not depart without fulfilling it. If there had been only one of them a physical ejection might have been a possibility, but with two it was just not on. Besides which, he still had that feeling of curiosity regarding the object of their mission. It was obvious that they wanted something from him and he might as well hear what it was. He could always refuse, could he not?

So in the end he said: 'Very well.' And he turned and went through a doorway into the kitchen.

It was not the most up-to-date and well-equipped of kitchens, and it was cramped for space. Penny had often complained about it. She said there wasn't room to swing a cat in it; but as they had never owned a cat, or any other kind of pet for that matter, Crane argued that it was hardly of any importance. The essentials were there, including a refrigerator.

It was to this that he went now and took out three cans of beer; one for each of the visitors and one for himself. He did not bother with glasses, for he felt sure Skene and

West were accustomed to drinking out of cans or bottles. This was something that Penny would never do; she said it was the equivalent of holding your table knife like a pen — vulgar. When Crane said that if this were so there had to be a whale of a lot of vulgar people around she said well of course there were. Hadn't he noticed?

⋆　⋆　⋆

Skene and West were sitting in two of the armchairs when he returned to the other room. They were smoking cigarettes.

'I see you've made yourselves at home,' he said.

'Sure. Why not?' West said.

Crane handed one of the cans of beer to Skene, who made a face as he took it.

'This the best you can do?'

'If you don't like it you don't have to drink it. What did you expect? Champagne?'

West accepted his can without remark, and Crane sat down on a sofa facing the other two. He drank some beer and watched them, waiting. They drank too, but said nothing.

'Well, let's have it,' Crane said. 'What's this all about?'

Skene took another swig, lowered the can,

looked at Crane and said: 'We got a job for you, soldier.'

'What makes you think I'm looking for a job?'

'Let's put it this way. You don't look to me like a guy what's rolling in wealth right now. So when somebody comes along and makes you an offer of a nice fat wad of the folding stuff just for a few days' work, how can you refuse?'

'And that's what you're doing? Making me that offer?'

'It's why we're here. No other reason. So what you say?'

Crane drank some more beer, looked at Skene, looked at West and said: 'You'll need to tell me more. Like how fat the wad is and what I'd have to do to earn it.'

'Take the second question first,' Skene said. 'You'd be needing to take a little sea trip in that boat of yours.'

'Ah!' Crane said. And now he could see where this was leading, and he was not so sure he liked the sound of it.

Skene drew smoke from his cigarette, let it out slowly and watched it drift towards the rather dingy ceiling.

'A trip across to Holland, shall we say.'

'With what purpose?'

'To fetch someone.'

'Only one?'

'That's right. Only one.'

Crane shook his head. 'I don't do that sort of thing any more. Like I said, I've retired.'

'Bullshit!'

West said: 'Retired on what?'

'That's none of your business.'

'You don't look like a bloke what's made a killing and don't need to work any more. Why ain't you down on the Riviera basking in the sun and living it up with all the other playboys and girls?'

'Maybe that sort of thing doesn't appeal to me.'

'And maybe you ain't got the means.'

'Maybe not. Makes no difference. I still don't do the kind of job you have in mind any more.'

'Now look,' Skene said. 'You haven't heard yet what the offer is. Don't you want to know?'

'You're going to tell me anyway. So get it off your chest.'

'What would you say to ten grand?'

It was certainly a lot more than Crane would have expected. He had brought a dozen passengers across for less than that. The boat had been pretty crowded but nobody had complained; they were only too pleased to be getting to the end of their journey. And this payment was to be just for the one. There had to be a catch in it somewhere.

'I'd say it's still no go.'

Skene gave a shake of the head. 'I can see you're playing hard to get. Okay, so let's say fifteen gees. How about that?'

It was a quick rise, and it was surely an indication of how important Skene and West rated the operation of bringing their man over from the Low Countries. It was obvious that he could be no ordinary illegal immigrant, and Crane wondered just how much the two men in suits stood to gain if the deal went through; and also how much they were prepared to cough up to ensure that it did.

When the bidding reached twenty thousand the thought came into his head that this would really be a nice round sum of money in return for a few days' work. He reflected also that he was undoubtedly in a rather poor way financially and could see no prospect of things improving on that particular front in the near, or even the distant, future.

So he said: 'This one you want brought over; I suppose it's a man?'

'Dead right,' Skene said.

'Well, it seems to me he must be a proper VIP if you're willing to pay twenty thousand pounds to bring him into the country. So what makes him so valuable?'

'Never you mind,' West put in. He seemed to be losing his temper and was maybe none too happy regarding the size of the offer his partner had made. Possibly it was somewhat higher than the figure the pair of them had agreed on beforehand as the upper limit. 'It's none of your business whether he's a VIP or a bloody nobody. You're just the ferryman. Right?'

'Wrong,' Crane said. 'I haven't said I'll do it.'

That was when they began to apply a bit of pressure.

'You better take the money,' Skene said. 'We could maybe make things bad for you else.'

'Is that a threat?' Crane asked.

'What's it sound like to you?'

'It sounds like a threat.'

'You're smart,' West said, sneering a little. 'Don't take you all day to pick up the message.'

'So how could you make it bad for me?'

'A word here and there in the right lugholes,' Skene said. 'We know a thing or two about you and your activities in the past. Why else do you think we'd be here?'

Crane believed he was bluffing. What he

was saying was that they had information about him which they could pass on to the police. He doubted, even if they had such information, they would want to have any dealings with the coppers. But he could not be sure; they might be vindictive enough if he refused to co-operate with them to do their damnedest to make trouble for him. And that was something he really did not want.

'Think about it,' Skene said.

He thought about it. And taking one thing with another he could see what a lot there was going for him if he accepted the offer of twenty thousand pounds sterling for a job he was perfectly capable of doing. It could be the last one. After that, with the money in his pocket, the future would take on a much brighter aspect. He might make it up with Penny and live happily ever after, as the old fairy tales used to end.

So he said: 'This twenty K. It'll be in cash?'

'What do you think?' Skene said. 'Would you accept a cheque?'

'I'd have to think twice about it. From you.'

He could not imagine this kind of business being done through a bank. Cash was anonymous, and secrecy was the name of the game.

'And it's payment in advance?'

'Now, now!' Skene said, and he looked pained. 'You know better than that. You know it ain't the way things are done. There'll be an advance, of course.'

'How much?'

Skene pursed his lips and seemed to be making a calculation in his head. Then: 'Say two down and the rest on completion of the contract. How do you like the feel of that?'

'I don't. The advance is too small.'

'But you'll be getting the lot eventually. So what's the difference? You won't need no spending money on the trip.'

'I'd still like more in hand. Five, say.'

'Three.'

They settled for four.

It crossed Crane's mind that when he had played his part and brought the passenger safely to England Skene and West might do the dirty on him and refuse to pay up. It was possible, but he doubted it. In these matters perhaps there was some honour among thieves. Moreover, Skene and West might want to do more business with him at some time in the future, and if they had bilked him once they were not likely to be given a second chance.

'Tell me,' Skene said, 'as a matter of

interest. How did you get yourself into this line of business?'

'It's a long story,' Crane said.

'And you're not going to tell it?'

'No, I'm not going to tell it.'

4

Mr Heathcliff

It really started years ago on the day he went up to London to seek his fortune. He had left the secondary modern where he had been educated at the age of sixteen with little in the way of educational achievement to fit him for a lucrative post in the great world outside. So the jobs he did obtain tended to be poorly paid and ephemeral. He was out of work for much of the time and was being continually badgered by his uncle, who was an auctioneer's clerk.

Uncle George was a skinny little man with a large moustache and an exaggerated idea of his own importance. He never tired of pointing out to Crane what a sacrifice he and his wife had made in adopting the orphan; a sacrifice for which the orphan himself felt little gratitude. From the first he had been treated as an interloper and compared unfavourably with Wilfred and Hector, the two cousins who had every encouragement to regard him as an inferior being. They were a few years older than he was, and when he left school they were already at university. So there he was living with an uncle and aunt who wanted nothing better than to be rid of him for good and all.

He was eighteen when he decided to make a clean break; to get away for ever from that hated terrace house in the small country town where he had been brought up; away from the man and woman who scarcely spoke to him except to complain of something or other that he had done or left undone. He just could not endure living there any longer.

Neither the uncle nor the aunt made any attempt to dissuade him when he announced his intention of leaving. He would have been surprised if they had.

'Where will you go?' Uncle George asked.

He answered without hesitation: 'London.'

'To make your fortune?' Aunt Edith said in the sneering kind of way she had when speaking to him. 'Like Dick Whittington?'

'Something like that.'

'You'll have to do a lot better than you've done here,' his uncle said.

'I intend to.'

He had no idea what he would do. He had never been to London, but he felt that there had to be opportunities for a young man like him. He would find something.

* ★ ★

Rather to his surprise when the time came for him to say goodbye Uncle George gave him a hundred pounds to help him on his way. Perhaps the old boy felt it was worth that much to be rid of this unwanted member of the family. Or maybe it was a way of easing any twinges of conscience he might have felt at allowing his nephew to go off on his own with so little preparation for what might lie ahead. He must have been aware of the pitfalls that lay in wait for any youngster venturing into the metropolis alone and inexperienced in the ways of the world; many of which could be very nasty ways indeed.

Crane, with all the confidence of youth, his entire luggage packed into one canvas holdall, climbed aboard the train that was to transport him from the place of his birth to that vast conglomerate which had acted as a magnet to so many before him and no doubt would continue to do so for thousands yet to come.

He had a few qualms during the journey. It could hardly have been otherwise. For all his youthful exuberance on setting out, as the train speeded along the rails, taking him into the unknown, there had to be moments when he questioned the wisdom of what he was doing. Had he been too hasty in abandoning the safety of the terrace house and setting recklessly out on this adventure? Ought he not perhaps to have waited a few more years when he would have been more mature? Maybe.

But then he banished such doubts from his mind. How could he have endured those extra years in that place with Uncle George and Aunt Edith forever nagging? What future could there have been for him in that dull provincial town? It had been imperative that he should get away. There could be no doubt about that.

Yet when the train reached Liverpool Street Station he was again a prey to some misgiving. There were such crowds of people, so much hurrying here and there, so much noise and bustle; and the place was so vast, it made him very much aware of his own insignificance. Could he really hope to make his way in a city to which this was no more than a gateway?

Once more with an effort of will he put such doubts behind him. It was now a little after midday and it seemed to him that the best course would be to take an initial look at London, or at least to some part of it.

With this object in view he handed his holdall in at a left-luggage office, bought a guide to the capital from the station bookstall and set out.

★ ★ ★

Eventually, in the course of his wandering, he came to Holborn and the City and thence to the West End with its glittering display of shops and theatres. He was entranced by it all, fascinated by Piccadilly Circus and Regent Street and Whitehall, which hitherto had been mere names to him. Later he found his way to the Embankment and saw for the first time that famous river which threaded its meandering way through the heart of London. To his right were the Houses of Parliament and to his left on the other bank and further upstream was the Festival Hall.

It was growing dusk now and lights were coming on all over the place, making a wonderland of the scene with their reflections in the water. But there was an autumnal chill in the air and he suddenly realised how hungry he was. He decided to go back to Liverpool Street, get himself a snack and then reclaim his luggage.

And then what? He ought to get himself accommodation somewhere before nightfall; perhaps at a cheap hotel. He would have to be careful with his money. Even with the hundred pounds that Uncle George had forked out his total capital amounted to little more than one hundred and fifty. How long would that last even with the strictest economy in a place like London where everything was so devilishly expensive? Not long; that was for sure. So it was imperative that he find himself a job of some kind without delay.

Back at the station he got himself a meal, and as he was leaving the refreshment room he almost collided with a man. He was rather an odd-looking individual; he was tall and thin and stooping and he was dressed all in black: black hat with a flat crown and wide brim, black raincoat, black trousers and black shoes. His face was horse-like, long and quite pallid, as though it had been preserved in a cellar away from the light. He put Crane in mind of an actor playing the part of a curate in a low comedy, though he was not wearing a dog-collar.

He moved aside to avoid the collision and gave a faint smile. Crane recalled seeing him earlier; he had been hanging around the bookstall when Crane bought his guide to London and might have been waiting for a train, though he had no luggage. But that had been some hours ago, and here he still was, still, it seemed, just hanging around.

Perhaps he had nothing better to do. Perhaps he was a jounalist picking up material for an article, a study maybe of the rich variety of travellers passing through this great railway station. But this seemed unlikely, and he did not look to Crane like a journalist, though he had to admit to himself that he had never met a member of the news-gathering profession and no doubt there were many varieties of the breed. Anyway, it was no concern of his and he had more important matters to think about; foremost of which was the question of accommodation for the night.

He collected his bag and found a seat where he could consult the guide regarding hotels and lodging-houses. There was a section devoted to this subject and the choice ranged from the grand hotels like the Savoy and the Dorchester, which were obviously quite out of the question for him, to boarding-houses in Bayswater and Blooms-bury. He was so absorbed in his study of the guide that he failed to notice that someone had sat down on the seat beside him until this someone spoke.

'I see that you are looking for a hotel.'

The remark, uttered almost in his ear, startled Crane. He glanced up and saw that the person who had spoken was none other

31

than the tall thin man in the black clothing whom he had noticed earlier. He had the kind of voice which Crane thought matched his appearance: the word that came into his mind was unctuous.

'Forgive me,' the man said. 'But I could not help noticing. Would I be mistaken in thinking you are perhaps new to London?'

'Yes I am, but — '

'Ah, I know what you are about to say. But what business is it of mine? Don't deny it.'

'Well — '

'Of course, of course. Quite a natural reaction. But the fact is I can possibly help you. And before you ask, quite naturally of course, why I should bother to do so, I will tell you it is my vocation, as you might say. My name, by the way, is Heathcliff.'

The name seemed to strike a chord in Crane's mind. Surely he had heard it somewhere before. The man appeared to read his thoughts. He smiled, and the smile was as unctuous as his voice.

'Think of Emily Brontë. *Wuthering Heights.*'

That was it of course. He had never read the book but he had seen more than one dramatisation on television. Surely it was Laurence Olivier who played the part in a film.

'No relation, of course,' the man said. 'As far as I know.'

Crane thought it was a stupid thing to say. How could he be related to a fictional character in a book? But he saw that the smile was on Mr Heathcliff's face again, so no doubt he had been making a little joke; one maybe that he was in the habit of making.

Then he said: 'Let me hazard a guess. You have come to London to make your fortune. Am I right?'

Crane said nothing.

'Possibly,' Mr Heathcliff said, 'you were unhappy at home and decided to move away and start a new life in famous London Town.'

Crane wondered whether the man was a clairvoyant. He had certainly been pretty well on target with his surmise.

Mr Heathcliff smiled again. 'You are not the first, and I fear you will not be the last. It has a fatal attraction for the young. Now let me tell you something which you may find hard to believe. There are men who keep a lookout for young fellows like yourself or even younger. How old are you, incidentally?'

'Eighteen,' Crane said. And immediately he had misgivings about revealing this information, though he could not have said why.

'Eighteen, eh? A delightful age. How I wish

33

that I — But let us not dwell on that. What is your name?'

Crane told him that too, again with some misgiving.

'Paul Crane, eh? Well, Paul, as I was saying, there are men who look out for youngsters just like you coming in from the provinces by train unaware of the pitfalls lying in their paths. These men batten on such innocents for their own evil purposes. Do you know what I should like to do with such people?' And here Mr Heathcliff crooked his long bony fingers and made as if he were wringing somebody's neck with his bare hands, looking quite fierce for the moment. But then he gave a laugh and relaxed and said: 'But I must not allow myself to become too melodramatic, however powerful my feelings may be. No doubt you have read about such villains?'

Crane had not. All he had read about in that sort of line was the scoundrel who had made off with David Copperfield's baggage and half-guinea when he was about to quit London on his way to Dover. And he doubted whether that was the kind of villainy Mr Heathcliff was talking about.

'Anyway,' Mr Heathcliff said, 'you are fortunate. I can help you. Of course you do not have to accept my assistance. You can just tell me to go away and mind my own business.' He paused, as though waiting for Crane to do just that; but when he got no response of any kind he went on: 'But the point is this: I run a hostel for youngsters like you. Numbers are of course limited, but at the moment a room happens to be available. The accommodation and catering are fairly basic, naturally, but adequate I think; yes, quite adequate. The hostel is run, not for profit but rather to help young people such as yourself. I would hesitate to call it a charitable institution, but perhaps it approaches that, in some respects at least. So now, Paul, are you interested?'

Crane hesitated. It crossed his mind that Mr Heathcliff might even himself be one of those villains he had been so vehement in condemning; that his anger regarding them was merely feigned, a bluff to present himself in a better light. But he dismissed the thought; it seemed too unlikely. And anyway, there could be no harm in seeing what the hostel had to offer. The strongest argument in favour of this was that it solved the immediate problem of shelter for the night and took a load off his mind.

So he said: 'Yes, I'm interested. I'll give it a go.'

After all, though Mr Heathcliff might look an odd fish, that was no proof that he was not sincere. So he would go with the man; he would spend the night at the hostel and in the morning, if things were not to his liking he would move on. He was a free agent, was he not?

'Good,' Mr Heathcliff said. 'Let us go then.'

5

Letterby House

They travelled by taxi. Mr Heathcliff said it was the most convenient way. Crane assumed he would be paying, though he might of course add the fare to whatever the charge for the lodgings might be. Mr Heathcliff had refrained from mentioning any precise figure for this, but from what he had said Crane had inferred that it would be less than that which might be charged by even the cheapest boarding-house.

He had no idea where they were going, but the journey seemed to be a very intricate one, involving much manoeuvring through heavy traffic and the turning of many corners. Crane was utterly confused, but the taxi-driver appeared to have no trouble at all in finding his way. He probably knew the maze of London's streets like the back of his hand.

Crane suddenly felt the pressure of Mr Heathcliff's hand on his thigh and became aware that the man was leaning towards him.

'No doubt, Paul,' he said, 'this is all very strange to you at present. But you will get used to it and you'll soon be able to find your way around. In a week or two we'll turn you into a proper Londoner.'

Crane was not sure he cared much for the implication that Mr Heathcliff was proposing to take him under his wing and teach him the ropes, as it were. And he was quite sure he had no liking for Mr Heathcliff's hand on his thigh. But he was reluctant to brush it off because he did not wish to offend the man. Fortunately, the hand was very soon withdrawn without the necessity for any action on his part.

'Soon be there,' Mr Heathcliff said. 'Not much further now.'

*   *   *

The street they finally came to was quite a short one, forming a link between two longer and more important thoroughfares. The house was at one end of a row. It was quite large but rather dilapidated, a fact which would have been more evident in the daytime than it was at this moment, illuminated as it was only by a nearby streetlamp. It was probably Victorian, and there was a short flight of worn stone steps leading up to the front door from a neglected piece of garden that was nothing more than a few square yards of rough grass, an overgrown shrub or two and a variety of weeds.

Mr Heathcliff paid off the cabman, pushed open a squealing iron gate and led the way to the front door, Crane following with his holdall. The door was not locked, which seemed odd, and Mr Heathcliff opened it and went inside.

'Come in, come in,' he said. 'Welcome to Letterby House. Why it is called that I have no idea. The origin seems to be lost in antiquity. Maybe there was once a Letterby who lived here, but who knows? It is of no consequence. It serves its purpose.'

They were in a fairly large entrance hall, from which a carpetless staircase curved away upward, rickety-looking banisters on one side. The floor was of bare tiles, rather chipped and worn down after years of wear from a multitude of boots and shoes, and a passageway led to regions where a kitchen might be expected to exist, and maybe a scullery and cellar.

In this direction noises could be heard, as though someone was engaged in certain culinary activities. The light in the hallway was provided by a low-power electric bulb suspended inside a rectangular shade of coloured glass. There was a chill in the hall which was far from welcoming and an odour of damp wallpaper.

'If you will follow me,' Mr Heathcliff said, 'I will show you your room. Do not expect luxury.'

It was up two flights of stairs and was certainly far from luxurious. Spartan might have been a more accurate description. It was an attic with a dormer window, bare floorboards that showed evidence of wood-worm and a dingy grey ceiling from which quite a deal of plaster had fallen away to reveal a patchwork of rotting laths.

The furnishing consisted of an iron bedstead, a chest of drawers with a swivel mirror on top and one rickety chair with a rush seat.

In years gone by Crane guessed that a maidservant had occupied this attic and had worked long hours for very little pay. In those days a candle would have provided the illumination; now at least there was electric light, although it was a bare bulb suspended from the ceiling. It was cold in the room, and here, as in the hall, there was that curious odour of dampness and decay.

'The bathroom,' Mr Heathcliff said, 'is on the next floor down. You will have this room to yourself.' He made this sound like a rare privilege. 'Most of our lodgers share rooms.'

'I see,' Crane said. 'And how much would I — '

'How much will you have to pay? Is that what you're asking?'

'Well, yes.'

'Oh, let's not go into that just now. Tomorrow we can work something out. If I were a rich man nothing would please me more than to provide everything free of charge — board, lodging, the lot. Alas, I am not rich and I have to make ends meet. You understand?'

'I suppose so.'

Mr Heathcliff stroked his chin, looked at Crane in a speculative sort of way and said: 'You have some money, I suppose?'

Crane admitted that he had.

'As a matter of interest,' Mr Heathcliff said, 'how much?'

Crane hesitated. He was not sure he wanted to reveal the state of his finances to this man. Why should he?

Mr Heathcliff noticed his reluctance and said: 'Of course you do not have to tell me. It's entirely up to you. But it may help me to help you if I know more or less how you are situated in that respect. Do you see?'

Crane did not see; not precisely. But after all, what harm could there be in giving the information? So he said: 'I've got a little more than one hundred and forty pounds.' And then he felt he had been a fool to confide so much to someone he had met for the first time only an hour or so earlier.

Mr Heathcliff gave a fleeting smile. 'Quite a sum, quite a sum. But not, I fear, enough to last for long if you don't soon obtain some kind of employment. Just for the present though, I think it might be advisable if you were to allow me to take care of it for you. I hate to have to admit as much, but there are a few members of our little community who are not altogether to be trusted. Light fingered, one might say. I would keep the money in my safe, and you could call on me for any you might require from time to time. What do you think of that?'

The idea did not appeal to Crane at all. He preferred to keep the money in his own pocket. He did not believe the risk of someone stealing it from him was as great as Mr Heathcliff was making it out to be. He was probably exaggerating.

'I think,' he said, 'I'll hang on to it.'

A frown appeared on Mr Heathcliff's face, but it was gone in a moment, and he was as unctuous as ever when next he spoke.

'Of course, dear boy, if that's the way you feel. Far be it from me to try to persuade you against your wishes. However, might I suggest a small advance would not come amiss now that we are on the subject of money.'

It seemed to Crane that this was a very quick turnaround on Mr Heathcliff's part. Previously he had dismissed any talk of financial matters as something that could wait until the next day. Now he appeared to have changed his mind.

Crane said nothing; just waited for him to go on. Which he did.

'I would suggest thirty-five pounds. Does that seem reasonable to you?'

It depended, Crane thought, on what the amount was supposed to cover. If it was the rental for just one night of the attic room it was pretty steep to say the least. But perhaps it was intended to include meals and maybe more than one night; advance payment for a protracted stay perhaps.

But did he want his stay at Letterby House to be protracted? He was not at all sure that he did. He would be in a better position to make a decision on that point when he had been rather longer than less than half an hour in the place. Certainly his first impression of it was not exactly favourable, but he was not looking for anything very grand, and at least it would be a base for operations while he hunted round for some profitable employment.

So he said: 'That would be for more than one night, would it?'

Mr Heathcliff smiled benignly. 'Why, of course, dear boy. You surely do not imagine I wish to make a profit from you. No, no, no. Not at all, not at all. You must not misjudge me, Paul.'

But he did not say how many days of residence the advance was intended to cover. And Crane hesitated to press him on this point. He remembered too that that there was a taxi fare which Mr Heathcliff had paid. So perhaps on the whole thirty-five pounds was not an excessive amount. He took out his wallet, extracted three tenners and a five and handed them to his host.

'Now,' Mr Heathcliff said, 'leave your bag here and come with me. I'll give you a guided tour of the house to make you feel at home. Let's go.'

He led the way and they went down the stairs with Mr Heathcliff pointing out on the way the bathroom, which was hardly the kind you saw advertised in the glossy magazines but was much in keeping with the rest of the place, and the doors to the other bedrooms. On the ground floor he indicated a door which gave access to what he called his sanctum; in other words his office. He opened the door for only a moment or two, and Crane got just a glimpse of a comfortably furnished room with armchairs and book-cases and a kneehole desk with a litter of papers and a telephone on it. Then he was whisked away and led down the passageway to a large old-fashioned kitchen where a grossly fat young man was busy with the preparation of a meal.

'This is Rupert,' Mr Heathcliff said. 'Our chef. Rupert, let me introduce our new lodger, Paul Crane.'

The so-called chef grinned at Crane. He had a face like a very large dumpling, round and pink-cheeked and shining with sweat, produced no doubt by his physical exertions and the heat from a gas cooker. On his head was a white chef's cap and his bare arms and pudgy hands emerged from a rather grubby singlet like overgrown roly-poly puddings. An equally grubby white apron was stretched across his ample stomach and on his splayed feet a pair of ancient trainers with no laces seemed in imminent danger of slipping off.

'Pleastermeecher,' he said. 'You gonna be here for the evenin' meal?'

Mr Heathcliff answered the question. 'Of course he will be. There'll be enough for one extra mouth, I hope.'

'Sure. No problem. Always plenty to spare, Mr H. Nobody goes to bed hungry in this establishment. Not if I can help it.'

Judging by Rupert's girth, Crane could well believe this, even though Mr Heathcliff was himself no advertisement for the abundance of the food at Letterby House. But some people remained thin however much they ate; they were like the lean kine in Pharaoh's dream.

'We have dinner here in the evening,' Mr Heathcliff explained. 'Most of the lads are out all day, you see. Some call it supper. It's all the same.'

★　★　★

They went next to what Mr Heathcliff called the common room. This was furnished with a number of chairs of various kinds, an old sofa, a plain deal table and some shelves of dog-eared books and magazines. There was a television set in one corner; a rather old one, quite unlike that which Crane had spotted in the sanctum, which was large screen and possibly stereo.

There was only one person in the room when they went in, and he was watching a cartoon film on the television.

'Switch that rubbish off, Charlie,' Mr Heathcliff said. 'I want you to meet our new member, Paul Crane.'

The youngster did as requested, stood up and took an appraising look at Crane. He was stockily built, possibly five feet six in height, with close-cropped hair and a face that could in no way have been described as handsome. He had a wide mouth and a nose that looked as though someone had pressed it with a thumb while it was still new and malleable. He had in all a puckish look, and there was about him a certain air of shrewdness and worldly wisdom far beyond his years. All in all the impression Crane had was of a kind of artful dodger.

'Hi!' he said. And he grinned. 'Welcome to Liberty Hall.'

'This,' Mr Heathcliff said, 'is Charlie Green. If he doesn't know everything that's worth knowing he certainly thinks he does. I will leave you two to get acquainted with each other while I attend to some other matters. I am sure Charlie will fill you in with regard to the routine of the house.'

He turned away and left the room.

'So,' Green said when the door had closed behind Mr Heathcliff, 'you're the new boy. Where'd the Bishop pick you up?'

'Bishop?' Crane said.

Charlie Green winked. 'That's what we call him around here. He's got these manners like he was some big nob in the church. The way he dresses an' all. Fact is he's the biggest bloody hypocrite on two legs.'

Crane was surprised to hear this; though perhaps not quite as surprised as he might have expected to be. It was more the bluntness of the statement than the content that struck him. He had already begun to have doubts regarding the genuineness of Mr Heathcliff's philanthropy, and Green was merely confirming these doubts.

'What makes you say that?'

'Oh,' Green said, 'you'll see. You probably think it was all out of the goodness of his heart that he picked you up. Where was it?'

'Liverpool Street Station.'

Green seemed mildly surprised. 'Liverpool Street! That's a change. It's usually St Pancras or Euston. Kids coming down from the north and that. Maybe he was getting too well known there and thought he'd better try a different patch.'

'But you're not a northerner, are you?'

'Me! Do I sound like one?'

'I wouldn't have said so.'

'And you'd be right, mate. I'm from the Smoke. Good old London Town. I wasn't picked up on no railway station.'

'No?'

'No,' Green said. But he did not say where

48

he had been picked up, and Crane did not ask.

'You'll be in the other attic, I 'spect,' Green said. 'I'm next door. Pretty rough quarters, but it ain't so bad really. At least you get the place to yourself. The others, they all share rooms on the next floor; maybe three or even four to a room. They're welcome to that. You lookin' for a job?'

'Well, yes. I've got to make a living somehow.'

'Could be hard. You got any money?'

'Some.'

Green gave a laugh. 'But not much, hey? I bet the Bishop asked you that. I can see by your face he did. Did you tell him how much?'

Crane admitted that he had done so.

'And he offered to take care of it for you, no doubt.'

'Yes, he did. But I said I'd rather keep it myself.'

'Wise man. Once you let him get his paws on your cash you can say goodbye to it. Nobody ever got anything back from him; not that I heard of. Got sticky fingers, he has. Did you pay him anything? Like rent say.'

'Yes. Thirty-five pounds.'

Green whistled softly. 'All for a bloody attic.'

'Well, it was by way of an advance. Board and lodgings.'

'So you're planning to stay on?'

'I don't know. I wasn't really, but — '

'I suppose you could do worse. It's better than a cardboard box in a shop doorway.'

Green had mentioned the kind of awful prospect that Crane tried not to contemplate. If nothing turned up would he eventually find himself out on the streets? It could happen.

'What,' he asked, 'is the normal rate for an attic?'

'Don't know,' Green said. 'I don't pay none.'

'You mean Mr Heathcliff lets you have it free?'

'Nah. He ain't that generous. The thing is, I pay in kind.' Crane was about to ask what he meant by this, but there was an interruption as the door opened and two more young men came into the common room. Green introduced Crane to them, and after that some more drifted in and he never got round to asking the question.

6

Sweet Dreams

There were twelve of them at the dinner table, with Mr Heathcliff presiding at the head. There was a serving hatch between the kitchen and the dining-room, through which Rupert passed the dishes. He apparently ate by himself in the kitchen.

Without his hat Mr Heathcliff could be seen to have lank black hair to match his clothes. At this time in the evening dark stubble had begun to appear on his chin and his hollow cheeks, above which the bones were prominent. At the summit of his cranium was a bald patch like an inverted saucer.

Before anyone began to eat he lowered his head, made an arch with his fingers and said grace.

'For what we are about to receive may the Lord make us truly thankful.'

Crane caught Charlie Green's eye across the table. Green gave a wink and silently mouthed the word: 'Hypocrite.'

The first course was a stew, with

dumplings, boiled potatoes and brussels sprouts. The stew was tasty and plentiful, and it was followed by apple pie and custard. Crane thought it was as good a meal as he had had in quite some time. Rupert's cooking beat Aunt Edith's by a mile.

Conversation round the table was carried on in a number of regional accents: Midlands, North Country and even Scots. Mr Heathcliff was a benign presence, a kind of father figure presiding over his family. Crane wondered whether Charlie Green's assessment of him was correct. Perhaps the young man was biased; perhaps he had for some reason or other got on the wrong side of Heathcliff and took a jaundiced view of him as a consequence. It was possible, but Crane was inclined to believe what Green had said. He was glad he had not agreed to let the Bishop take care of his money.

★   ★   ★

After the meal most of the youngsters returned to the common room; though a few left the house to seek entertainment elsewhere. Green informed Crane that anyone was free to come and go as he pleased, but there was a curfew at eleven o'clock when the doors were locked.

'So what happens if someone is back late?'

'Just too bad for him.'

'He's not allowed in?'

'No.'

'That's tough.'

'It's the rule. And the Bishop is hot on rules. Still, there's always ways and means, ain't there? That there Rupert, he's got a few duplicate keys to the back door. He had them made, and you can get a loan of one at a quid a time. That's if you have a quid to fork out.'

'Suppose you haven't and you're still late. What then?'

'Then if you ain't got nowhere else to go you can kip in the old summerhouse in the back garden. It's all right in summer but cold as charity in winter. And the roof leaks. I wouldn't recommend it.'

Crane wondered whether Green was speaking from experience. It was possible. For his part, he decided to respect the curfew. That was if he stayed on at Letterby House.

Some of the youngsters were watching television, but some others were playing cards at the table. The game appeared to be nap, with pretty low stakes apparently. This was hardly surprising, since anyone who had money to throw away would certainly not be living in that sort of place. He wondered how they all managed to scrape up enough of the wherewithal to pay even for this accommodation.

He noticed that a few of them were smoking, but the cigarette was being handed from one to another, which seemed a pretty extreme economy measure.

Then Green said: 'You fancy a joint?'

It was then that he realized that it was not tobacco that was being smoked but cannabis. He could smell it now, and he recognized the odour. He had in the past tried the stuff himself but had never cared much for the effect. The first time or two it had simply made him feel sick.

'Does Mr Heathcliff allow that in here?'

Green laughed. 'Betcha life he does. Where you think the lads buy the grass?'

'Oh, come on,' Crane said. 'You're not telling me he's a dealer.'

'That's just what I am telling you. And you better believe it. Moreover it's not only hash. Speed, ecstasy, you name it; he can get it for you. But he draws the line at the real hard stuff — coke, big H and that like. My guess is he's afraid somebody might snuff it on the premises. Then he'd really be in the shit, with a dead body on his hands.'

Crane found it hard to believe. But then he gave the subject some more thought and it became easier. You came across some odd characters in the world, and Mr Heathcliff not only looked odd but was odd. He wondered what else of the unexpected he would learn about the Bishop if he stayed on at Letterby House long enough.

Charlie Green was watching him with a faintly amused expression on his gnomish face.

'Stick around,' he said, 'and there's no telling what you'll find out. You've come to a rum sort of place here, I can tell you. There's some odd characters in it, and the oddest of the lot by a long chalk is the guy what runs it.'

★　★　★

Crane was tired both physically and mentally after his first day in London; so he did not stay up late. By ten o'clock he was in bed. It was cold in the attic room and a wind had come up which rattled the casement window and flung some heavy drops of rain to patter on the glass. The mattress on the iron bedstead was hard and lumpy, and when he moved he could hear the springs protesting. The sheets were chilly, and now that he was in bed he no longer felt sleepy; there was so much material running through his mind, so many impressions of this day that had marked a turning-point in his life.

And then he began to think about the little slavey who perhaps in years gone by had occupied that room. What a life of drudgery hers must have been: up at the crack of dawn, raking out the cold ashes of fires and lighting them afresh, carrying hot water in big jugs up to the bedrooms, emptying slops, cleaning boots and shoes, polishing brasses and furniture, scrubbing floors, black-leading the kitchen range, always at the beck and call of maybe tyrannical employers — and all for what? Her board and a miserably few pounds a year in wages.

He slept at last and had weird dreams in which Mr Heathcliff, dressed in a cassock, with a bishop's crook in his hand and a mitre on his head, figured prominently. He awoke to find sunlight creeping in through the dormer window. The rain had ceased, the wind had dropped, and there was every promise of a pleasant autumn day.

7

Ambitions

Breakfast was at eight o'clock; a good solid meal starting with porridge. Charlie Green told Crane he believed that for some of the lads this and supper were the only meals they had. Judging by the way they tucked in Crane thought this could well be true.

'What do they do all day?' he asked. 'Do they have jobs?'

'Search me,' Green said. 'I never ask. Wouldn't surprise me if some of 'em did a bit in the begging line. And there's Nobby — that's the one with the guitar — he works the subways and such. I come across him now and then and I seen people dropping the odd coin in the titfer he's got lying on the ground beside him, so I'd say maybe he don't do too bad. Mind you, he's quite a dab hand at plucking them old strings, though I don't go much on his voice when he does the singing bit. Sounds like he's got a pain in the gut or something.'

Rather to his surprise Green invited Crane

to go along with him when breakfast was finished.

'That's if you ain't got nothing else planned.'

Crane had not. The fact was that now he had made a clean break from his former way of life and was actually in London, this city of his dreams, he had no idea of what his next move should be. He ought, he supposed, to start looking around for a job of come sort; but where did you start? In a place the size of this there must surely be thousands of jobs available if you knew where to look for them; but he did not know. And maybe there were thousands of applicants for them anyway, probably far better qualified than he was.

So when Green made the offer he accepted it without hesitation. He got the impression that the youngster had taken a liking to him. Which was rather odd, since he appeared to have no particular friends among the other lodgers. Indeed, he seemed to regard them with a certain contempt, perhaps because he was a native Londoner and felt himself to be a cut above them, and a deal smarter.

When they left the house Crane noticed that his companion was carrying a large canvas bag with a shoulder strap. The bag appeared to be empty, and he wondered what it was for. But he refrained from enquiring.

No doubt he would eventually discover its purpose.

'Anywhere special you want to go?' Green asked.

Crane could think of nowhere. 'I really ought to be looking for a job.'

'Run away from home, did you?'

'Not exactly. I've been living with an uncle and aunt. My parents died when I was just a kid. Car accident.'

'It happens. This uncle and aunt turf you out?'

'No, nothing like that. I wanted to leave.'

'Why? Didn't you get on with them?'

'Not very well.'

He had a feeling that he was telling Green too much about himself. But what did it matter?

They were walking down the street on which Letterby House was situated, and when they came to the corner at one end they turned to the right and continued on their way. Crane was content to let Green do the guiding. For this one day he would abandon the idea of looking for a job and just go where his companion led him.

Suddenly Green said: 'Did the Bishop try to get into bed with you last night?'

Crane was startled. The question had been so unexpected. He wondered whether Green could be joking, but there was no smile on his face. He appeared to be quite serious.

'Get into bed with me! Whatever makes you ask that?'

'So he didn't?'

'Of course not.'

'He will,' Green said. 'Give him time. Good-looking young guy like you. He's bound to be trying it on very soon. You can bet on that.'

Crane thought about this. And then he said: 'Are you speaking from experience?'

'Sure.'

'He tried it with you?'

'That's right.'

Crane was silent, and they walked on without saying anything for a while. Then Green said: 'All right. I know what you're wanting to ask. What happened? Did I let him?'

'Well, did you?'

'Nah. What you take me for? I told him to get to hell out of it, else I'd stick a knife in his guts just to see if he'd got any blood in him. He got the message and he ain't tried it again. Not with me, that is.'

'Would you have done it? Stick a knife in him, I mean.'

'Maybe. If I had a knife. What's the odds? He believed it and it made him back off.

Didn't make me one of his favourite blue-eyed boys though. I think he'd like to kick me out, but he don't dare try it. He's afraid I might go to the coppers and spill the beans on him. And there's plenty to spill, believe you me.'

'And you'd do that?'

'Go to the cops? What me? Leave it out. I steer clear of that lot. But of course he don't know that, so he don't dare do anything to set me against him. I may leave one of these days anyway. I think it's getting to be about time I made a move.'

Crane was giving some more thought to what Green had told him. Then he said: 'So he hasn't tried it on you any more. But do you think he has with any of the others?'

'Wouldn't surprise me. Of course none of them has a room to hisself, but there'd be nothing to stop him inviting one of them to his quarters, would there? And there's some mightn't object to pleasing him — for a consideration.'

Again Crane detected that note of contempt in Green's voice. It was quite apparent that he had a low opinion of the other residents in Letterby House. Possibly this was one of the reasons why he was thinking of leaving.

* ★ ★

They came to a bus stop and boarded the first bus that came along. Green paid the fares.

'Your turn next time,' he said.

It suited Crane. He was pleased to let Green take him where he would. For the present he was relieved of the responsibility of making any decisions for himself. Moreover, he was curious to discover how the young man occupied his time when he was away from Letterby House.

After they left the bus they walked for quite a way until they came to a large supermarket with a spacious car-park that was about three-parts full.

'Wait for me here,' Green said.

Crane saw that he had taken a pair of cotton gloves from the bag he had been carrying and he was putting them on. Then he started making his way in among the parked cars. Crane lost sight of him at times, but then his head would appear again, though it was impossible to see what he was doing. And then after a few minutes, he was back.

'Let's go,' he said. 'But don't hurry. Just take it nice and easy, so's not to attract attention.'

Crane began to question him, but Green

would have none of it. 'Not now, Paul. Later. Just keep walking.'

They were well out of sight of the supermarket when he gave a laugh and said: 'Some people, they just make it easy for you, they're so damn careless.'

He had taken off the cotton gloves and Crane saw that the canvas bag was no longer empty; there was a bulge showing that there was something in it.

'Maybe it's you, Paul, bringing me luck. You're a talisman, that's what you are. I better keep you with me. First thing in the day and it's a hit. Fifth boot I try isn't even locked. All I have to do is open it and help meself. They don't come better than that.'

'Are you telling me you stole something out of a car boot?' Crane said. He could hardly believe what he was hearing. And Green was so cool about it, so matter of fact, as though it was all in the day's work. As perhaps it was for him. 'You just stole it?'

'Ah, come on,' Green said. 'Let's not talk about stealing. That's a word I never use. Things left lying around, I just help myself to them.'

Crane wondered whether he ought to walk away from Green right then and never have anything more to do with him. Green was a crook; small time perhaps, but a crook nevertheless. And he, Paul Crane, was associating with him. So that made him an accessory, did it not? Yes, he really ought to walk away now and dissociate himself from such a companion, who might draw him into real trouble.

But he did not walk away. He felt a kind of pleasurable excitement. Somehow the very audacity of the act set his pulse racing. So did this mean that he himself had a certain leaning towards dishonesty? He had never thought so. But the fact was that he had never thought at all about that particular subject.

So now he did not condemn Charlie Green out of hand for what he had done, and apparently was in the habit of doing. Indeed, he felt a certain admiration for the impudent way he had carried out the operation. It took nerve to do what he had just done. Charlie Green had nerve; that was certain.

'What you going to do about it?' Green asked, casting a faintly mocking glance at Crane. 'You thinking of handing me over to the filth? Bringing the law down on me. Is that what you have in mind?'

'No,' Crane said. 'It's just that you took me by surprise. I never guessed — '

'Of course you didn't. You're an innocent, aincher? But a guy's gotta make a living somehow, ain't he?'

'Yes, but — '

'But why don't I get a proper job? Well, for one thing it ain't that easy. You'll find out if you try. And this way I get to be my own boss. Nobody to kick me around, see? I'm a free agent, Paul boy; free as air. You get what I'm saying?'

'Yes, I can see all that. But what about the future? You can't go on for ever pinching things from cars.'

'You got a point there,' Green admitted. 'But I don't mean to. I got ambitions. I'm going up in the world, I am.'

He did not say how he intended to achieve this ambition, but he seemed confident that a time would come when he would be a man of substance. And maybe he would. His confidence was such that he even had Crane half believing him. For the moment.

8

No Laugh for the Bishop

They were sitting on a bench in St James's Park, basking in some early autumn sunshine like gentlemen of leisure when Green showed Crane what was in the bag. It was a Bosch cordless electric drill, and it must have been brand new because it was still in its carton.

'Now that,' Green said, 'should pay the rent for a day or two. It'd set you back maybe thirty nicker in a shop, I'd say.'

Crane thought this might be so, though he had little idea of the price of electric drills, having never bought one. But he did see a snag, which he now pointed out.

'But you've got to sell it, haven't you? Can you do that?'

Green gave a wink. 'No problem.' He put the drill back in the bag. 'No problem at all. I know a man who'll take it. And I'll tell you where he lives. A place called Letterby House.'

Crane stared. 'You mean Mr Heathcliff?'

'None other.'

'Well, well, well!'

He seemed to be learning more and more about the Bishop almost by the hour. Not only was he a hypocrite, a dealer in illicit drugs and a sexual pervert, now it appeared that he was also a receiver of stolen goods: obviously a man of many parts, and none of them very savoury.

'Not,' Green said, 'that he's a pukka fence, but my guess is he knows somebody who is. I'd say he passes the hot goods on pretty damn quick. That way he don't get caught in possession if the coppers ever get round to giving the place a going-over.'

'You think they're likely to?'

'You never know, do you? The drawback to dealing with him from my point of view is I don't get such a good price for my merchandise. I'm thinking of giving him a miss one of these days and going straight to the other guy.'

'But how will you manage that? I mean Mr Heathcliff isn't likely to tell you who he is.'

'No matter. There's others in the market. I'll find somebody. I know a few people who might point me in the right direction. I get around and keep my eyes and ears open.'

Crane could believe this.

★ ★ ★

They spent the rest of the day just drifting around, with Green acting as a guide. Having made the one early pick-up he seemed to regard this as enough for one day; the rest of the time was free. They lunched in style on burgers and fries at a McDonald's and they went to a cinema when they were tired of walking. They were back at Letterby House in time for whatever Rupert had to offer for the evening meal.

Mr Heathcliff was at home, and Green went straight to his sanctum with the electric drill. When he rejoined Crane in the common room he was seething.

'The old bastard!' he confided to Crane, keeping his voice low so that no one else in the room could hear. 'He would only give me five quid. Five lousy quid! I ask you! Well, that settles it. No more goods for the Bishop. Not from me. I'll go find somebody what's an honest dealer.'

Which was rather a contradiction in terms, Crane thought, bearing in mind the kind of person he was talking about. But he did not say so.

* * *

Several days passed and Crane had not yet found a job. The fact of the matter was that he had not been looking for one with any great dedication. All he had done was glance through the classified advertisements of vacancies in a newspaper and conclude that none of the jobs on offer was quite the thing for him. Most of his time had been spent going around with Charlie Green and being instructed in the finer points of pilfering from cars and shops without being spotted by spy cameras or store detectives. Bag-snatching was not in his repertoire; he drew the line at that. He regarded bag-snatchers, especially those who preyed on elderly women, as the lowest of the low; in a word, scum.

'You gotta have certain standards, ain't you? Meanter say it's nasty, ain't it? Besides which, you can get caught running off. And the bag might not have anything in it to make it worth the aggro anyway. See what I mean?'

Not that he was doing terribly well in his own line. He was having a thin time with the cars, and most of the stores seemed to be too well guarded to risk lifting anything from them. The result was that he was getting a bit short of cash and Crane was paying rather more than his fair share of the expenses. The drain that this put on his small amount of capital was causing it to shrink at an alarming rate, and he could see no real prospect of halting this shrinkage. It bothered him a little;

in fact somewhat more than a little; but when he mentioned this to Green he was told not to worry.

'You get times like this when nothing seems to go right. Then, hey presto, things look up. Happens all the time.'

Which might possibly have been his experience, but it failed to dispel Crane's feeling of anxiety.

'Something will turn up,' Green said.

'Well, I hope so. Because the Bishop will be looking for some more money from me for board and lodgings.'

'Sod the Bishop,' Green said.

And that was the way matters stood until an occurrence that brought things to a head rather more quickly than either of them had been expecting. Though in fact it was something that Green had predicted. Mr Heathcliff paid a visit to Crane's attic bedroom late one night.

Crane had been asleep, and he awoke to discover a hand probing under the bed-clothes. It was a shock, and not a pleasant one. The fingers felt cold on his skin and he could hear someone breathing heavily, apparently leaning over him so that their two heads were quite close together.

He gave a yell and got an arm free and struck out blindly with his clenched fist. The fist made contact with some part of the other person's body. He heard a gasp and the groping fingers were pulled away.

Then a voice said: 'Now, now, Paul; there's no need for violence.' And it was Mr Heathcliff's voice, as unctuous as ever. 'It's only me. Don't be alarmed, dear boy. You have such a fine young body. So nice and smooth the skin is. Quite delightful.'

Then the fingers started groping again and for the moment Crane simply froze. He just could not believe what was happening, even though Charlie Green had warned him. It was so far outside his experience. Nothing like this would ever have happened in Uncle George's house; not in a million years.

Mr Heathcliff was still uttering soothing words and the fingers were creeping lower. Crane was galvanized into action and struck out again. This time he knew precisely where his fist had found its mark in the darkness; it could only have been Mr Heathcliff's rather prominent nose, no doubt about it. The man gave a cry of pain and must have staggered backwards, away from the bed.

At that moment someone opened the door and switched the light on. It was Charlie Green, barefooted and wearing only a singlet and briefs.

'Well now,' he said. 'What have we here?'

It was a question that required no answer, because it was quite apparent what they had there: they had Crane sitting up in the bed with tousled hair and the master of the house standing in all his stringy and unattractive nakedness with blood streaming from his nose.

And then Charlie Green began to laugh, and after a moment or two Crane joined in the laughter. The only one of the three who did not laugh was the Bishop. Possibly he did not appreciate the comic aspect of the scene. Maybe he was standing in the wrong place.

★　★　★

He did not put in an appearance at the breakfast table. There was a report going around that he was indisposed, but it was only Crane and Green who were aware of what had caused that indisposition, and they were keeping the information to themselves.

They left the house with their luggage soon after breakfast, having informed Rupert that they would not be returning to Letterby House and asking him to pass this information on to Mr Heathcliff.

'Where are you going?' Rupert asked.

'Who knows?' Green said. 'The wide world is calling and we have to go.'

Rupert grinned, and with a face like his it had to be a large grin. 'What you're saying is you had a set-to with the Bishop and he's kicked you out. Right?'

'Wrong. He didn't kick us. We kicked him.'

'Same difference,' Rupert said. And then: 'Baby, it's cold out there. And you won't have me to cook for you.'

'That's just what we're looking forward to,' Green said.

But Rupert was right, Crane thought. It could be cold out there.

★　★　★

It was hard going at first. Often they were sleeping in pretty rough places and wondering where the next meal would be coming from. But they stuck together; where there were two of you it was never so bad as being on your own.

They could have got help. There were the Social Security people. No one had to starve. But they would only have taken this step as a last resort.

'Once you get yourself mixed up with that lot,' Green said, 'you're finished. You've lost your freedom. It's all form-filling and that. They've got their hooks in you. It's as bad as being known to the police. Well, almost.'

'And you aren't?' Crane said. 'Known to them, I mean.' It was a question he had never asked before, and he put it now with some hesitation, not sure how Charlie would take it. But there had been no need for concern on that point.

'Nah,' Green said; and he gave a wink. 'I've had a few narrer squeaks but I've never had my collar felt.'

Crane knew more about his comrade's background now. His mother had never been married, but she had had a swarm of kids by various fathers. Green never knew who his own was; the man had departed before Charlie was born. He had been neglected from the start; and when he was not neglected he was hammered, either by his mother or the man she was living with at any particular time. He had run away from his home in the East End as soon as he could fend for himself and he had been fending for himself ever since. With his mother he had lost all contact, and according to his own account he never wished to see her again.

'She was a bitch, a proper bitch. And still is, I reckon. They don't grow out of it, do they? She drank, you know. Half the time she was sozzled. Then she'd scream at you and cuff you round the lughole if she got near enough to you.'

Crane reflected that, unhappy as his childhood had been, it could not have been nearly as bad as Charlie's. It was small wonder that he had no desire ever again to get in touch with his mother.

★   ★   ★

Even when the clouds were darkest Green remained cheerful. He was always hopeful regarding the future.

'Things'll look up soon, Paul. You'll see.'

And he was right. They did. He found a fence to take the stuff which he could no longer place with Mr Heathcliff. And, as he had foretold, he got better prices for the goods.

Crane was still little more than an assistant, an apprentice to the trade, as it were. It was Green who had the skill to pick things up here and there, while he acted as lookout and a carrier for the loot. He no longer had any qualms regarding the illegality of what the pair of them were doing; sometimes he was himself surprised at the ease with which he had come to look upon this mode of life as perfectly acceptable and not to be condemned. So was he just naturally lacking in a social conscience, as Charlie Green undoubtedly was? Perhaps he was.

They found a bed-sitting room to let in a seedy old house in a row in the Plaistow area. It had had a lot of previous tenants, all of whom seemed to have left their mark as a contribution to the dinginess of the accommodation; but as Green remarked, it was a sight better than a kip on a concrete bed underneath the arches.

9

Joy-Ride

One day he suggested that they should take a car and go for a joy-ride.

'Make a change.'

'Can you drive?' Crane asked.

'Why, sure I can.'

'And you've got a licence?'

'Nah. But what's the odds? How about you?'

'You mean can I drive?'

'Yes.'

'As a matter of fact, I can.'

He had worked for a time at a garage. It was one of those jobs he had that didn't last; about the only one he ever enjoyed. He found that he had a natural gift for the work; it really appealed to him. That was when he learnt to drive; he picked it up in no time at all. But he had never taken a driving test and never had a full licence.

He might have stuck at that job if it had lasted; but when he had been there for about six months the garage went out of business and he was out of work again. That was when he decided to pull up stakes and try his fortune in the big city.

'Right then,' Green said. 'As it's a nice day we'll get ourselves a car and maybe go for a drive into the country. It'll be fun, and I've heard the air out there is good for you.'

Crane thought it might also get them into trouble, driving around in a stolen car. But he did not say so. Charlie seemed dead keen on the idea, so why not? It would certainly make a welcome change to the city life, and for the moment they were not pushed for cash.

*   *   *

The car they took was a Ford Escort. It was not very new and it was standing on the forecourt outside a suburban railway station. It was still early in the day, so the odds were that the owner was a commuter who had gone to work in the City or some such place and would not be back to reclaim the vehicle until much later.

Crane had ceased being amazed at the ease with which Charlie could break into a locked car. Usually he did it to get at the radio or something left on the rear seat. Sometimes, of course, an alarm was set off, and then they would beat a hasty retreat; but it was strange how little notice people took of car alarms, except when the car was their own. In this case there was no alarm and no steering-wheel locking device, so there were no problems. Charlie had a metal strip he used for dealing with the lock, and he was a dab hand at starting the engine without an ignition key. He called it hot-wiring. Crane wondered who had taught him these techniques, for they were not the kind of skills that would just come to you naturally.

Within minutes they were in the car and had it moving away from the forecourt with nobody yelling at them to stop or even taking the least bit of notice. They were both wearing gloves, because Charlie said it was as well not to leave fingerprints all over the place, when you were doing something with a touch of illegality about it.

'Neither one of us has got his dabs on police records, and it's best to keep it that way.'

Crane just hoped they would continue to keep their prints unavailable to the enforcers of the law, but he knew that one day this might not be possible. He tried not to look that far ahead but just to live for the present.

They drove northwards into the Essex countryside, heading for nowhere in particular and keeping as much as possible to minor roads. Crane did some of the driving, and he liked the feel of it. It had been a while since he had been behind the wheel of a car and there was a sense of exhilaration in the exercise. One day perhaps he would have his own car and use it whenever he wished; but he had to admit that the prospect of this seemed pretty dim at the present time.

Later they changed seats again and Green drove. It was all quite aimless; driving for the sake of driving and taking a wandering course with no special destination in mind. It was a lovely day and there was petrol in the tank that someone else had paid for. What more could one desire?

★   ★   ★

They came to a village. It was the picture-book kind, with a green, willow trees, a pond with ducks swimming on it, thatched houses in the background. Charlie stopped the car by the pond.

'Now this,' he said, 'is real nice. One of these days I may come and live in the country. Away from all the hustle and bustle. All the aggro.'

'Never,' Crane said. 'You're a city boy. You'd die of boredom.'

'Well, it's a thought.'

'And that's all it'll ever be. Of course if you

were to get stinking rich you might have a big country house with an estate and a place in town too. You could bring the birds down for weekends and that. Swimming-pool and all the trimmings. But it's just a dream, of course.'

'Nice to dream sometimes,' Green said. 'You hungry?'

'Now that you mention it, yes, I am.'

'There's a pub over there. Maybe we could get a meal.'

It was on the other side of the pond; an old building that might have stood there for centuries. They could just make out the sign: The Nag's Head.

'Do we walk or take the car round?' Crane said.

They were still thinking about this when the police car appeared on the scene. It was a panda with one policeman in it.

'Oh, oh!' Green said. 'This could be trouble. Let's hope he goes past.'

The hope was vain. The panda car came to a halt about ten yards from the Escort, facing it on the same side of the road. The driver got out and walked towards them. He was young, with a cherubic face under his peaked cap. He looked scarcely older than the two in the car.

'Let me do the talking,' Green said.

81

The policeman came to his side and peered in over the lowered window.

'Is this your car, sir?' he asked.

It was the first time Crane had ever heard anybody address Charlie as 'sir'. He doubted whether it was a favourable omen.

'No,' Green said.

The policeman seemed rather taken aback by this blunt reply, and Crane wondered just what line Charlie was taking.

'So you borrowed it?' the policeman said.

'No.'

'Hired it perhaps?'

'No.'

The policeman appeared to be getting slightly nettled by these replies. Maybe he thought Green was taking the mickey. Which was what it seemed like to Crane. It was crazy.

'May I see your driving licence, sir?' the policeman asked.

Green shook his head. 'Sorry, officer. Haven't got one.'

'Then why are you driving a car?'

'I'm not driving it,' Green said.

'You're in the driving seat.'

'That's so. But me and my friend here are just waiting for the owner to come back.'

'Why wait for him in the driving seat?'

'I wanted to see what it felt like. Some day

I may have a car of my own.'

Crane doubted whether the policeman was swallowing this story. He might be young but he was hardly likely to be as gullible as that.

'What is your name, sir?'

'Harold West,' Green said.

The policeman had his notebook out now and he jotted it down. Then he looked past Green at Crane.

'And your name, sir?'

Crane had had time to think up an answer, and he said without hesitation: 'Frank Smith.'

He thought the policeman might ask for their addresses too, but he did not — for the present. He went round to the front of the car and it looked as though he was making a note of the number. Then he went back to the panda and appeared to be using the telephone.

'He's getting on the blower to the station,' Green said. 'If the car's been reported stolen we're in the cart. Get ready to make a run for it.'

But when the policeman came back it was obvious that he had not obtained any information of that kind. He looked faintly disappointed. He asked where the owner of the car had gone.

It was Green who answered. 'He said he

was going to the pub over there to make a telephone call.'

'How long ago was that?'

'Just before you arrived.'

'And what is his name?'

'He didn't tell us. We was walking along and he pulled up and asked if we'd like a lift. So we hopped in.'

'And then when he went away to make this telephone call you moved into the driving seat?'

'That's right.'

He did not believe it. Crane felt sure of that. But he also had a feeling that this young and possibly inexperienced policeman was uncertain what to do next. He gazed across the pond at the public house and said: 'He's taking a long time making that phone call.'

'Well, maybe he decided to have a drink while he was there, and a bite to eat as well, if they do that sort of thing.'

Again the policeman cast a glance at Green which seemed to ask the question whether he was being smart. But Green's face was expressionless.

Finally the policeman lost patience. 'Wait here,' he said. 'I'm going to see what's doing over there.'

He went to the panda and locked it, then

strode away in the direction of the public house.

Crane and Green watched him until he disappeared inside. Then Green said: 'Come on, Paul. Let's scarper before he comes back.'

Crane needed no urging, and the pair of them left the car and started walking rapidly away from it, resisting the temptation to break into a run. They reached a bend in the road and were soon clear of the village, and the policeman had not yet reappeared.

'You think he'll chase us in the panda?' Crane said.

'Maybe. But he won't know which way we've gone. It'll just be guesswork.'

'He could guess right.'

'You worry too much,' Green said.

But it seemed that he was a trifle worried himself, for when they came to a field gate with a meadow on the other side he suggested climbing over it and taking cover behind a hedge which bordered the road. They were only just in time, for a moment later they heard a vehicle approaching, and peering through the hedge they saw it go by at considerable speed. It was the panda car.

'What now?' Crane said.

'Now we wait. He won't go far. He'll know if we've gone this way he'll soon catch us. When he doesn't he'll reckon we took the other direction and he'll come back.'

He was right about that. There was not much traffic on the road. A tractor hauling a trailer with a load of baled straw went past, followed by a lorry, and then the panda car appeared again. They gave it time to get well out of sight, and then they climbed back over the gate and started walking.

'The question now,' Crane said, 'is how do we get back to London? It must be miles and miles, and we don't even know where we are.'

They had already decided that returning to the village to pick up the Escort was out of the question. The policeman had taken the number and now he would be certain the car had been stolen. Other officers would soon be on the lookout for it.

'We shall just have to use public transport,' Green said.

'What public transport? I don't see any.'

'The trouble with you, Paul,' Green said, 'is you always look on the black side of things. Something's bound to turn up.'

What turned up first was a sudden downpour of rain. The fickle English weather had let them down and they had no coats and nowhere to go for shelter. In minutes they were soaked to the skin. They tried thumbing a lift but drivers simply ignored their signals, probably not liking the look of them. They had walked nearly ten miles before they found their way to a small town from which there was an infrequent bus service to Chelmsford. At Chelmsford they eventually caught a slow train to London, and they arrived back at their quarters very late in the evening, damp, tired, hungry and with blisters on their feet.

It was, as Green sourly remarked, the end of a perfect day.

Crane decided that joy-riding was not all it was cracked up to be. He noticed, too, that Charlie Green seemed to have lost all enthusiasm for the idea of buying an estate and going to live in the country. He never mentioned it again.

10

Dead Easy

Two years later Paul Crane and Charlie Green were still together, but things were looking considerably better for them. They had a steady job and were earning pretty good money.

They had also left the dingy room that they had formerly occupied and were living with two girls, Vera Gray and Kimberley Thorne, in a basement flat rented by the girls.

It was certainly no luxury apartment and it was not in the best part of London, but as Charlie said, it was not bad, not bad at all. Of course, after what he and Crane had been used to almost anything that was not downright rancid would have been an improvement. And even for a place like that the rent was as much as the girls could afford, and maybe a bit more at times. So they were happy when Crane and Green came along to share the expenses, and a few other things besides.

They had run across one another in a discotheque, with the music hammering in their ears and the lights weaving glittering patterns around them. It was a kind of hothouse for instant relationships; and none could have been more instant than theirs. They went back to the flat together, and next day Crane and Green moved their gear into their new home.

They told the girls they were in the used car business; which was true enough, seeing that the steady job was stealing cars. This piece of information they felt would be best kept to themselves; it was not something they wished to spread around. And anyway, Vera and Kimberley were not inquisitive regarding the precise nature of the business. They accepted Paul and Charlie at face value. And they seemed to like the faces.

* * *

It had been a chance meeting in a public house that brought about a change of fortune for the two young men. The public house was down the East End way and was filled to capacity. There was a darts match taking place at one end of the bar, and there was some pop music being pumped out to add to the general hubbub, above which could be heard the cry of the referee calling out the score. The air was thick with cigarette smoke and beer was being consumed by the gallon.

Crane and Green were wedged in a corner at the end of the room furthest away from the place where the darts were flying. They had no interest in the contest, and neither apparently had another young man who was almost rubbing shoulders with them.

'Darts!' he said in a tone of disdain. 'Listen to them. They're going crazy. You'd think it was a football match.'

This remark seemed to be addressed to Charlie Green, so he said: 'You a football fan?'

'I watch it.'

'Live or TV?'

'Both. When I get the chance.'

'What club?'

'Spurs. Ever since I was a kid. You?'

'Actually,' Green said, 'I'm Arsenal.'

'Ah well,' the young man said, as if being magnanimous regarding another person's weakness, 'we can't all be perfect, can we?'

He was short and rather plump, with a face that had a lardy appearance, and he had a straggling wispy beard that seemed to be undernourished. His hair was of a mousey colour and was beginning to recede. His voice was soft and rather low-pitched, so that to hear what he was saying above the general clamour Green and Crane had to bend their heads towards him in a conspiratorial manner.

The conversation, having touched on the subject of football, remained there for some time, and the respective merits and weaknesses of Tottenham and the Gunners were discussed in detail. Crane, having no burning interest in either club, merely put in a word here and there.

The plump young man informed them that his name was Percy Bateman. He insisted on buying pints for Crane and Green. And then Green bought a round, and after that Crane did the same. It was then Percy Bateman's turn again, and tongues were being loosened and discretion evaporating in a warm alcoholic haze.

'I got a job on cars,' Bateman confided. 'Dagenham way.'

'With Ford?' Green asked.

'Not on your life. No production line for me. Not on new cars neither.'

'In a garridge like?'

'Well, in a way. You know anything about cars?'

'Do we know anything about cars! Percy, you're looking at two of the best drivers around.'

'Is that a fact? So what you drive?'

'Anything that's going. Anything we can lay hands on.'

A warning bell started ringing in Crane's head. Charlie was talking too much. It was the beer that was doing it. And it could be dangerous. But how was he to be stopped?

Bateman screwed up his little piggy eyes and stared at Green. 'Are you saying what I think you're saying?'

'Depends, don't it?'

'On what?'

'On what you think I'm saying.'

'Well, it sounds to me like you might be in the car-snatching game. I may be wrong. But I hope I'm right.'

'Now why,' Green said, 'would you hope that?'

'Because if you are I know a man you might do business with.'

★   ★   ★

It just went on from there. It was two days later when Percy Bateman took them to see the man. The man's name was Arnold Landers, and his place of business was a large one-storey concrete building with a corrugated asbestos roof. It looked as though it might once have been a small factory or a warehouse, but the work that was done in it

92

now was on cars: good modern cars that strictly speaking had never been in any need of the attention; a fact to the truth of which their legitimate owners would undoubtedly have attested if they had been given the chance.

The work was carried out very promptly on the cars as soon as they arrived, so that in a very short space of time they had new number plates and were a different colour. Certain other changes were made to them, so that very soon they had acquired quite a new identity. Equipped with forged documentation these stolen cars departed to find their way into the hands of new and unsuspecting owners either in the United Kingdom or abroad.

As a front to this activity there was a certain amount of legitimate repair work carried on in the place, and no doubt account books could be produced if required. But the real money spinner was the other line: the stolen car transformation operation.

And at the head of this nefarious business was Mr Arnold Landers, a man in his early fifties; tall, elegant and undoubtedly handsome. He had black hair with just a touch of grey in it, keen eyes, aquiline nose, thin-lipped mouth and a trim military moustache, also greying. One might have put him down as a retired army officer, member of one of the better London clubs perhaps. The voice supported this impression; upper class accent without doubt.

In fact it was all a sham. He was the son of a Hammersmith butcher. He had indeed for a short while served in the army, but had risen no higher than the rank of lance-corporal before persuading his father to buy him out. He had for a time been an actor, and a reasonably competent one. It was during this period in his career that he had acquired the accent and attached it to the physical attributes with which nature had endowed him. But on the stage he never became more than a small part player, just as he had been in the army. So this too he had given up and turned instead to a life of crime, which he saw as a more likely way of enriching himself.

For some years he had been a confidence trickster, battening mainly on gullible women of a certain age who fell for his undoubted charm, and parted all too easily with considerable amounts of cash before he made a precipitate departure from their lives.

It was a man named Fulcher who introduced him to the car-ringing racket. Fulcher had the know-how but he lacked capital. Landers happened to be in the money at that time but had become tired of the confidence game and was looking for some alternative activity. So the two of them set up in business, trading under the name of Lanful Engineering. Fate soon stepped in to remove Fulcher from the partnership after little more than a year. He had a massive heart attack and died at the wheel of his car while kerb crawling in the vicinity of Euston Station. The surviving partner shed no tears. He was now sole boss of the show.

★　★　★

'So,' Landers said, staring hard at Crane and Green, 'you're the two bright lads Percy has been telling me about.'

Crane wondered just what Bateman had told him. It could not have amounted to much, since he had got little information from them apart from the fact that they knew how to steal cars. But apparently he had recommended them to the boss, and it seemed that Landers was ready to take them on. Apparently he had recently lost a couple of his suppliers; they had been picked up by the police for some crime quite unconnected with cars and were now out of circulation for a time.

So it was that Landers needed fresh blood in the organization and Crane and Green appeared to fill the bill. Thus it came about that they got their regular job.

★   ★   ★

They still worked as a pair, though it was Green who was the dab hand at breaking into the cars and getting them started. Crane did most of the driving, because there was no doubt that he was better at this than his partner.

They would pick the cars up at various places, always looking for models for which Landers had most demand. Often they would work late at night when there were quiet residential streets lined with parked cars from which they could take their pick. Other times Landers would ask for something special like a Jaguar or a Bentley, which you were unlikely to run across in the less affluent regions. For these you might have to look further afield, where the big houses of the wealthy citizens were situated. Charlie said he liked taking their cars best of all, because he knew they could afford to lose their property, and most of them were probably crooks anyway.

'How else would they get to be so stinking rich?'

'Now you're being cynical,' Crane said.

'No, I'm being realistic.'

There were days when things just fell into their hands. People were so careless, it was hardly believable. Like the time when they picked up a nice new Aston-Martin at a big Georgian house where there was a party in full swing. They could hear the music being belted out and the laughter and the shrieks of delight from the women who seemed to be having a whale of a time, and it was a certainty that nobody inside was giving a thought to all the expensive machinery that was parked on the gravel at the front of the house.

'My God!' Green said. 'Ain't they just having themselves one hell of a party. We oughter take all these cars because that lot in there'll be as pissed as arseholes and not nearly fit to drive when they start for home. It'd be acting in the interests of the general public.'

Which was good reasoning; but of course taking all the cars was out of the question. They had to be content with just the one. And there was this Aston-Martin with the door unlocked and the key actually in the ignition, just asking to be pinched.

'Some stupid cow with not much in the brainbox must've left it like this,' Green said.

'Ain't we the lucky ones!'

Crane drove. The car was not hemmed in by any of the others and there was not a sign from the house that anyone had noticed their departure. The journey down to Dagenham at that late hour was made without incident, and they got a bonus from Landers because he was so pleased with the car. In two days maybe it would be on the Continent with a new owner.

Sometimes it was like that. Dead easy.

11

Suspicion

They were still living in the seedy bed-sitter even though the money was coming in very nicely. The fact was that they hesitated to move into superior quarters because of a superstitious feeling that this might be tempting fate. But when the chance of sharing a flat with two charmers like Vera and Kimberley came along they had no qualms about grabbing it straightaway.

Yet all they knew about the two girls at that time was that they were young and lovely and had no attachments. It was a crazy way to start such a relationship; it was surely bound to hit the rocks almost immediately. Yet, oddly enough, it did not.

Facts concerning Vera and Kimberley were gradually revealed. It appeared that the major part of their income came from stints as go-go dancers; but this could in no way have been described as regular employment. Intermittently they did engagements for a kissogram agency; which they said was good fun but not particularly lucrative. All in all they were living pretty much on the brink, and the money went out as fast as it came in — if not even faster.

It occurred to Crane that maybe they had been on the lookout for some help with the cost of living, and he and Green had seemed like the answer to the problem. But he did not care. Vera was the girl of his dreams and Green seemed just as taken with Kimberley. That way it worked out perfectly for both of them.

As Charlie said: 'Paul, my boy, we've landed on our feet here, and no mistake. It may not last. Nothing ever does. But let's make the most of it while we've got the chance.'

To Crane this seemed an excellent idea. He wondered whether he was in love with Vera, and he wondered whether she was in love with him. Perhaps. And again perhaps not. Did it matter? Did you need some word like that for what they felt for each other? This irresistible mutual attraction. Why not take it for what it gave and hope it would not turn sour. At least not for a long, long time.

'You know,' Green said, 'in a way they're like us, them two. They're misfits. Or, as you might say, outcasts from society. See what I mean?'

Crane did see. Because they knew now a

great deal more about these two young females they were living with. The information had gradually emerged as confidences were exchanged.

One day Vera said: 'You know where me and Kim first met?'

'No,' Crane said. 'But I have a feeling you're going to tell us.'

'A remand home.'

'Is that a fact!' Green said. 'So you're bad girls really.'

'We absconded twice,' Kimberley said.

She sounded quite proud of this, as if it were an achievement of some kind. Maybe she thought they should have had medals for it.

They had both come from bad homes and had been taken into care at an early age. In effect they had no families and they had become allies in a fight against all those members of the community whose duty it was to exert authority over them.

'Know what you are?' Green said. 'I'll tell you. You're rebels.'

'Maybe so,' Kimberley said. 'And what are you two?'

'Oh, we're the same. You'd be surprised.'

'And maybe I wouldn't,' she said. 'Maybe I think there's more to you two guys than meets the eye.'

'Well,' Green said, 'you could be right at that.'

They still had not revealed just what kind of jobs they had in the used car business. Without actually saying so they managed to give the impression that they were salesmen; but it was all rather vague. Crane wondered whether some day Charlie might reveal the true state of things; he tended to be rather garrulous at times, and goodness knew what he might confide to Kimberley when their heads were on the pillow.

Not that the girls were likely to go running to the coppers and filling their ears with the information. They would not regard it as their duty as decent upright citizens to report any breach of the law that might come to their knowledge, because they were hardly in that category themselves. Still, it was best that they should be unaware of the car-stealing activities, because as long as they knew nothing about these they could not in any circumstances reveal anything.

★ ★ ★

Crane and Green never went to see the girls doing their go-go routine. It was not that they really disapproved of this activity, but they had no wish to observe a lot of other men getting an eyeful of what they felt ought by rights to be reserved for their delectation only. Yet they could hardly raise any objection. This was the way Vera and Kimberley had been earning at least a part of their living before the young men had even known of their existence, and it would have been unreasonable to expect them to abandon it now. Besides which, there was the financial aspect of the matter to take into consideration: it was income they could not afford to lose.

Later in the course of their relationship Green had cause to suspect that there was another source of income which neither of the girls had seen fit to reveal. He mentioned his suspicion to Crane.

'I believe Kim is on the game. Maybe Vera too.'

Crane was startled. This possibility had never occurred to him. Green, however, admitted that he had always had some doubts about the two; though he did not think they ever brought any clients to the flat even when he and Crane were not there.

'You got any evidence?' Crane asked.

'I saw her in a car with some well-dressed guy. Looked rich, oldish. Expensive car.'

'Did she see you?'

'I don't think so.'

'Well, it's not much to go on, is it? I mean there could be plenty of reasons why she was in the car with a man.'

'Could be. But me, I got a suspicious mind. And you have to bear in mind them girls have been living a dodgy sort of life.'

'That's true. So what are you going to do about it?'

'Nothing. What can I do?'

'You could tell her you saw her with this man in a car and ask her what she was doing with him.'

'And you think she'd tell me? She'd just get mad and tell me to mind my own bloody business. And I don't want to get on the wrong side of her when things are all so nice and cosy.'

'You could be wrong anyway.'

'Sure I could. And I hope I am. But I been thinking. If she and Vera are doing a bit of free-lancing in that line they're taking a risk. They may be stepping on somebody's toes. Some pimp may get to thinking they're poaching in his territory, and pimps can turn nasty. They're pretty handy with the flick-knife or the Stanley, and they can ruin a girl's looks for good and all. I'd hate to think of Kim with her lovely face carved up.'

Crane thought Charlie was making a great deal too much of what was after all a very slim piece of evidence. And he was reluctant to accept the conclusion that his colleague had so quickly jumped to. He did not wish to believe it could be the correct one, especially regarding Vera.

He tried to put the matter from his mind; but it stayed there, nagging. He wished Charlie had kept his suspicions to himself.

12

A Team

One day Vera came up with a suggestion. 'Why don't you two boys take some time off from your jobs so's we can all go for a nice car ride?'

And Kimberley immediately chimed in with her support for the idea. 'Oh, let's. It'd be great. Do let's do it. You have got cars, I suppose, being in the business and all?'

'Why, of course we have,' Green said, before Crane could get a word in.

'So how come we've never seen one? Where do you keep them?'

'Not here, that's obvious. There's no parking space.'

'Where then?'

'Oh, not far away. What's it matter?'

'So how about it?'

'How about what?'

'A car ride. The four of us.'

'Oh, I don't know.'

'Of course you do. Ah, come on, Charlie, it's a great idea. It'll be lovely. What do you think, Paul?'

Crane thought it was a thoroughly bad idea, not because he disliked the prospect of going somewhere with the girls but because he knew that if they were to go on this proposed excursion it would have to be in a stolen car, since neither of them had one of his own. And he remembered how things had turned out when they had tried something of the sort before. Suppose that kind of thing happened again while Vera and Kimberley were with them. It hardly bore thinking about.

So he said doubtfully: 'I'm not sure we could get the time off.'

'Oh, come off it, Paul,' Vera said. 'You don't work every day of the week. How about a Sunday?'

'Well — '

And Kimberley said: 'Where I'd really like to go is up the Thames somewhere. Maidenhead, say. I've never been there. Have you, Charlie?'

'No,' Green said. 'Can't say I have.'

'You, Paul?'

'Nor me neither.'

'And I bet Vera's never been there, so it'll be a new experience for all of us. I've heard it's a nice place.'

'You're talking like it's all arranged,' Green said.

'Well, it is, isn't it? You're not going to back out now, are you?'

Green gave a wry smile. 'Seems like we got no choice. How about you, Paul?'

Crane shrugged. It was like Charlie said; they had no choice. Unless they were willing to have a stand-up row with the girls. And who wanted that? Nevertheless, he remembered how that other pleasure excursion had ended: the walk in the rain, the blistered feet and the slow train back to London. And it bothered him.

He spoke to Green in private later. 'We must be crazy. You know what happened last time.'

'Sure I do,' Green said. 'But it'll be all right this time round. You know what they say: lightning never strikes twice in the same place.'

'I know that. But we're not talking about lightning, are we? We're talking about the lads in blue, the Old Bill.'

'Paul,' Green said, 'as I've told you before, you worry too much.'

★ ★ ★

It was the kind of spring day you dream about: sunny, not too hot but pleasantly warm. The car they had managed to pick up was a Renault; not very new but in good condition. Green told the girls it was his. He did the driving with Kimberley sitting beside him and the other two in the back.

They avoided the motorway and took a roundabout route to Maidenhead via Ealing and Uxbridge and Beaconsfield. They had lunch at a roadside cafe and arrived in Maidenhead in the afternoon. They parked the car and strolled down to the river which was looking its best in the sunshine.

There were a lot of boats of various sizes coming and going, some motor-propelled, others rowed by young men, bare-armed, bending their backs and showing their muscles.

'You ever done any rowing, Charlie?' Kimberley asked.

'Have I ever done any rowing! Why, I was in the Sea Scouts when I was a kid. Rowing, sailing, navigating; I done the lot.'

It was the first Crane had heard of this, and he doubted whether Charlie would have recognized a Sea Scout if one had come up and shaken hands with him. But he made no remark and let it pass.

Kimberley seemed quite impressed. 'Why Charlie, you're a real sailor. And I never knew.'

Green smirked; he seemed to be enjoying

himself. 'One day, when I get rich I'll buy me a yacht and do some real grand sailing. Down to the Med and that.'

'And take us with you?'

'Betcha life, Kim, betcha life. Put in at all the posh places on the Riviera — St Tropez, Cannes, Monte Carlo. Have ourselves a rare old time of it.'

'Sounds marvellous,' Vera said. 'I just can't wait.'

Dreams, Crane thought, just idle dreams. None of them really thought they would ever come true. Life was not like that. Not for people like them.

Then Kimberley said: 'Why don't we hire a boat and let Charlie take us for a row?'

And Vera said: 'Oh yes, that would be fine.'

But suddenly Charlie seemed to have lost interest. He said it was getting late and it was about time they made a start on the drive back to the Smoke.

'Some other day perhaps.'

Things took a turn for the worse when they went to pick up the car where they had parked it. It was still there, but there was a policeman standing beside it. He had a notebook in his hand and he was speaking into a mobile phone.

'Oh, oh!' Crane said. 'The lightning has struck twice.'

He and Green came to an abrupt halt, and the girls halted too.

'What you mean?' Vera asked. 'What's all this about lightning? There's no thunderstorms around.'

'That's what you think,' Green said. 'Let's get outa here. But don't run. Just take it nice and easy. Come on.'

'Why?' Kimberley demanded, not moving.

'Don't ask questions,' Green said. 'Just move it. Right?'

He had taken her arm and was forcing her to get into step beside him; moving away from the parked car, away from the man in blue who seemed to have taken an interest in it.

Crane spoke to Vera: 'Let's go.'

She seemed to have quickly come to an understanding of the situation and did not argue. The four of them began walking away from the car. The policeman was still talking into his mobile phone and appeared not to have noticed them.

'Now where are we going?' Kimberley inquired.

'We're going to find the railway station,' Green said.

'What for?'

'To get a train back to London.'

'I don't get it,' she said. 'What's wrong with

the car?' And then suddenly she did get it. 'Don't tell me. It's hot. That's why the copper was interested in it. Oh my!'

She came to a halt, and the others stopped too. They were out of sight of the parked car and the policeman now. There were plenty of people milling around, but they were minding their own business.

'Now look — ' Green said.

'I am looking,' she said. 'I'm looking at you, Charlie. And what do I see? I see a man what daren't go and pick up his car because it just don't belong to him. He pinched it, that's what. Now tell me I'm wrong.'

'Keep your voice down,' Green said. 'Do you want all the world to hear what you're saying? And let's get walking.'

They started moving again, and Kimberley lowered her voice. But she was still working on the same theme as fresh ideas seemed to come into her head.

'Know what I think? I think the pair of you are in this together. In the used car business, you said. I bet you are. What do you say, Vera? Have we or have we not been consorting with a couple of dyed-in-the-wool crooks who steal cars for a living?'

'I'd say you're right,' Vera said. 'They really took us in.'

'So what you think we ought to do now?

Hand them over to the fuzz?'

'Maybe it's our duty,' Vera said. 'Here's us thinking they was a couple of decent honest citizens, and what do we find? That we've been harbouring a pair of proper villains who might have slit our throats any day.'

She began to giggle, and Kimberley joined in.

'Now leave it out,' Green said. 'You know you're not going to do anything of the sort. You wouldn't want to get involved with that lot any more than we would.'

They did some more of the giggling, and Crane had a feeling that they were really enjoying themselves; delighting in this revelation regarding the true nature of his and Charlie's employment.

'Why, they're no better than we are,' Kimberley said.

'Did we ever say we were?' Green asked.

'Maybe not in so many words. It was just an impression you gave.'

'So now,' Crane said, 'are you going to kick us out or what?'

'We'll have to think about that, won't we, Vera?'

'Yes, we will.'

Crane was not much worried. He felt sure there was no prospect of their being turned out of the flat. He was pretty certain that the truth about the way he and Charlie made a living had come as no great shock to the girls. They had taken it in their stride.

And in the event there was never any hint of the four of them splitting up. In fact relations between them were, if anything, even better than before.

'We're a team,' Vera said. 'It's us against the world. Isn't that so?'

'It's so,' Crane said.

But he wondered just how long it would last.

13

Departure

It lasted almost a year. All this time life was so good that Crane could never shake off the superstitious feeling that it could not last. Something just had to go wrong.

And in the end something did; something more horrible than anything he could have dreamed about in the worst of nightmares.

It was one of those days when he and Green arrived back at the flat very late. They had picked up a car in North London, Highgate, a prosperous-looking residential area. It was a BMW in good condition, and they took it down to the garage with no trouble at all. There was always someone on duty there to let them in whatever the time; and after they had delivered the car they made their way home by public transport, which could be a bit dodgy at that time of night. You could get yobbos on the Tube ready to give you a hard time and maybe relieve you of your loose cash. But none of them ever gave him and Charlie any trouble. Possibly they could see they would have had a tough job on their hands if they had tried anything.

As usual the two of them arrived back at the flat on foot. The street was deserted and presenting that rather eerie appearance which such streets did late at night; like some scene out of a French film noir. They came to the iron railings guarding the steps down to the front door, and they could see no light showing in the window.

'I wonder,' Green said, 'whether they're home yet.'

There could be no certainty of that, because quite often the girls worked pretty late too. It was something that had always worried Crane a little, for there was no telling what might happen to them on the way home in a place like London — or, for that matter, any other town these days. Even with the two of them together they could still be in danger. But once when he suggested it to them they dismissed the idea out of hand.

'We can look after ourselves,' Vera said. 'We've been doing it practically all our lives and we're still alive to tell the tale. Nothing bad ever happened to us. Not real bad.'

'There's a first time for everything,' Crane said. And what he was thinking was that one day maybe they just would not get back to the flat. They would not simply be late; they would be missing. But there was nothing he could do about it. Whatever he might say they would carry on just as they had been doing long before he even knew they existed.

Green went down the steps first, but when he put his key in the door he found that it was not locked.

'That's odd,' he said. 'Looks like they are home and forgot to lock the door. Careless of them. Anybody could've walked in.'

It was then that Crane felt a chill in the blood. Because it occurred to him that somebody might have done just that. Uninvited.

Green pushed the door open and they went inside. There was a tiny entrance hall, and it was dark in there. Crane closed the door behind them while Green was feeling for the light switch. He found it and the light came on. There was no sound in the place except that which they themselves were making. Again Crane felt that chill in his veins and a sense of foreboding.

They went into the living-room. Green switched the light on in there too. There were two bedrooms in the flat, doors to them on the right. A door on the left gave access to the kitchen.

There was no one in the living-room.

'Must be in bed,' Green said. 'Sound asleep, I reckon.'

But Crane had spotted something that Green had not noticed; something he would have given the world not to have seen. He pointed a finger, and the finger shook.

'Look at that.'

It was on the white-painted door of one of the bedrooms. It could have been a smear of paint; but they both knew it was not that. They knew by the colour of it, which was red.

'Blood!' Green said. And then again on a rising note: 'Blood! Oh, my God!'

The door was slightly ajar. The smear looked as though it could have been made by a bloody hand grasping the edge. It was just above the knob, and one could discern the print of splayed fingers. It must have been a big hand.

Crane had to force himself to walk across to the door. He felt a great reluctance to go into that room which he shared with Vera, dreading what he might discover inside. But it had to be done. He reached the door. He touched it with his knuckles, avoiding the stain. He pressed on the wood and the door moved inwards with a faint squeaking of hinges that he had been meaning to oil for months and never had.

The door opened wide, and the bed was

there on the left. He saw it and gave a cry of anguish; a cry also of protest: 'No! Oh no!'

He heard Charlie Green's voice; Charlie at his side, looking at the same thing he was looking at.

'Jesus Christ Almighty!'

She was lying across the bed, on her back, her heels touching the floor. Vera, his lovely Vera, with the stab wounds in her chest and her blood staining the coverlet and the T-shirt she was wearing. Her eyes were open but sightless. Her face, untouched by the knife that had killed her, was deathly pale, the lips slightly parted, as though she were about to say something but had lost the script.

The two young men stood quite still for a few moments as if petrified by the grim sight; staring silently at the bed and the inanimate object lying on it. Then Green uttered a cry.

'Kimberley!'

He turned and rushed from the room with Crane following. The door of the other bedroom was closed. Green opened it and they looked inside. There was no one in the room.

'Maybe she got away.'

It was a faint hope, but he snatched at it desperately. Perhaps one at least of the girls had escaped the killer.

But the hope was vain. They found her in

the kitchen, where she had maybe taken refuge, closing the door but unable to hold it shut. She was lying on the floor, face down, and there were stab wounds in her back. There was blood here also; on her clothing and on the floor.

Green swore again, but Crane was silent. He stared at this second victim with a sense of disbelief. And yet he had to believe; the evidence was there and it was unmistakable. Vera and Kimberley were dead; murdered in their own home, where they should have been safe but were not.

The weapon that had been used, a knife or a dagger, was nowhere to be seen. The murderer must have taken it away with him. There was evidence of blood in the sink, which seemed to indicate that he had washed the blade under the cold tap. A damp tea cloth thrown aside had probably been used to dry it.

'Why?' Green said. 'Why? They never done nobody any harm and they was so full of life. And now the two of them, dead. It just don't seem possible.'

But it was more than possible. It was hard, cold fact.

'How did the bastard get in? They would never have left the door unlocked, would they?'

'Maybe they just forgot. Or maybe he rang the bell and one of them opened the door and he just rushed in. Maybe there was more than one. No telling.'

'But why? Who would want to do such a thing?'

'Could be like you said some time ago. A pimp got nasty because they were poaching his trade. Came himself to eliminate them, or sent an agent, a professional.'

'Or maybe it was a nutter, a crazy bastard with a grudge against go-go dancers. Saw their act, followed them home and just rushed in at their heels before they could even shut the door. But hell, what difference does it make? It's done and there's no way of undoing it. Now we gotta think of ourselves. This ain't our home no more and we better clear out pronto.'

'But what about them?'

Green shrugged. He had quickly regained his composure and had sized up the situation with cold logic. 'Nothing we can do for them now. They're dead meat and there's no way we're going to bring them back to the land of the living. This here's a part of our lives that's finished. We have to write it off and move on.'

'But shouldn't we call the police?'

Green stared at him in disbelief. 'Are you crazy? You know what'd happen? We'd be prime suspects, that's what.'

'But we didn't kill them.'

'Of course we didn't. But they might think we did and were just calling them in to prove how innocent we were. And even if they believed us there'd be a whole lot of interrogation and a bagful of questions asked about how we been getting a living and all that kinda thing. Just think about it. Do you want that?'

Crane did think about it, and he could see that Charlie was right. For people like them all contact with the police was best kept to a minimum; and that minimum ought to be no more than a nice round zero.

'I suppose you're right,' he said.

'You bet I'm right. Now we better get on with the packing.'

★ ★ ★

In fact there was not a lot of packing to do. They had never accumulated much in the way of fancy clothing and other possessions. They covered the bodies with sheets before they gathered their things together, and when the packing was done they went round wiping their fingerprints off anything they might have touched.

They switched off the lights before they left

and locked the front door behind them. There was no one around in the street to see them leave and only a distant rumble of traffic was to be heard. They reached a corner and turned to the right and went on walking. When they came to a drain they dropped the key through the grating. They would not be needing it again.

14

Parting of the Ways

Everything seemed to go wrong after that. They found new accommodation which was about on a par with that which they had had before moving in with Vera and Kimberley, but this seemed only to deepen the mood of depression that had settled on them since the gruesome discovery of the dead bodies. It affected the relationship between them too, and there was no longer that easygoing camaraderie in it that there had formerly been. The fact was, they were getting on each other's nerves.

They kept an eye on the news, searching for a report of the discovery of two murdered young women in a basement flat. But several weeks were to pass before anything of the kind appeared. It was the kind of area where there was little fraternising between neighbours. Residents tended to keep themselves to themselves and mind their own business. Vera and Kimberley had known no one else in the building and had made no attempt to make friends there. So no one reported that the two had not been seen for some time because no one even noticed their absence from the scene.

But as the weeks passed and the rent became due and was not paid, the landlord, a middle-aged Cypriot expatriot named Georghios Christofides, became rather impatient, especially when all his written demands brought no reply from his tenants. When his patience was exhausted, which did not take long, he visited the flat in person, and getting no result from the ringing of the doorbell, let himself in with his own key.

He immediately noticed the smell. He was, so he said, compelled to hold a pocket handkerchief to his nose before venturing beyond the lobby. When he had done so, the shock of discovering the source of the odour was such that he almost fainted. He got in touch immediately with the police, and he sincerely hoped they would soon apprehend the fiend who had done such a dastardly deed.

★   ★   ★

'It's as well,' Green said, 'that he didn't know about us being there. We'd have been up to our necks in it else.'

The girls had been careful not to inform

him of this. They said if he knew he would probably demand an increase in the rent; which was exorbitant enough as it was.

It apppeared that the police could get little information of any use from the neighbours. One woman said she had seen two young men going to the flat once or twice, but her description of them was vague and could have fitted almost anyone.

'I think we're in the clear,' Green said. 'They haven't got a thing on us.'

'That may be true,' Crane agreed. 'But they haven't got a thing on the bastard who knifed the girls either. And that I'm not at all happy about.'

'Well, you can't have everything. That's life, that is.'

Which was Charlie Green being philosophical; and bully for him. But Crane found it impossible to match him in that respect. He remembered Vera too clearly, and the pain was there and the anger, the resentment, and the sense of loss. It would be a long time before he could accept what had happened with any degree of resignation.

*   *   *

And then another blow fell. Arnold Landers was arrested and the market for stolen cars, as far as Crane and Green were concerned, vanished overnight.

It was a piece of good fortune that saved them from being caught in the bag as well. They were delivering their latest piece of merchandise when they spotted some police cars outside the premises of Lanful Engineering.

'Oh, oh!' Green said. 'This looks like trouble. Let's scarper.'

Crane was driving, and he made a U-turn and beat a quick retreat from the danger area. He half expected one of the police cars to give chase; but none came. It was dark at the time, but there was plenty of light where the police cars were parked, and maybe nobody was looking in the direction from which the stolen car was approaching. So they got away. But it had been a near thing.

They abandoned the car as soon as they felt they were a safe distance from the Lanful place. They felt it would have been tempting fate to go any further with it.

'We've been lucky,' Green said. 'But the luck could change. Best not to take any chances.'

They felt safe now. Nobody at the garage knew their surnames or where they lived; not even Percy Bateman. He had told them his full name, but they had been wary of revealing any more than was necessary. So to Arnold Landers and his lot they were simply Paul and Charlie. No one could give the coppers a lead to them even if they wished to do so.

'Just shows, don't it?' Green said. 'You can't be too careful. Never trust nobody; that's my motto. Present company excepted.'

★   ★   ★

But it was the end of the stolen car racket for them. Neither of them felt inclined to hunt around for another buyer, and in fact they both felt it was time for them to split up. There was that edginess in the relationship that had been increasingly evident since the murder of the girls, and they could not blind themselves to it. They had been together ever since that evening when Mr Heathcliff had introduced them to each other at Letterby House. But time moved on. They were more mature now and too often they failed to see eye to eye. Crane in fact had been ready to give up the car-stealing enterprise even before the decision to do so had been more or less forced on them.

Yet in the end it was Green who suggested the split. 'We got our own lives to live. We can't be in each other's pockets for ever.

We've had good times and bad, and we've pulled through. But now it's time to go our own separate ways, I reckon. What you say, Paul?'

'I think you're right. I've been thinking it for some time. Got any plans for the future?'

'Nothing solid. A few ideas. I'll get by. So will you.'

'Oh, sure.'

They were not entirely without capital. They had been prudent enough when the cash was flowing in to put some away for a rainy day. It was not in a bank or a building society but in cash, which was there for immediate use with no formalities. Now they divided it equally between them and prepared themselves for a new start in life.

So they parted and went their own ways and were to see each other never again.

15

Unhappy Note

Two years later Crane was acting as wheelman for a gang of criminals who specialized in robbing branch offices of banks and building societies, and now and then a sub-post office. He was not altogether happy in the work, but it paid well enough and he had no intention of going on with it indefinitely. Some day something better would come along; something even legal. But that day was not yet here.

All the getaway cars were stolen and were abandoned as soon as they had served their purpose. This part of the business was Crane's responsibility, and he was regarded as a pretty smart operator by the rest of the gang.

There were just three of them, and the leader was a forty-year-old ex-convict named Harry Bly, who had had a lot of experience and was a very tough character indeed. The other two members of the gang were about Crane's age and not terribly bright in his opinion. Without Bly to guide them and hand out orders they would have been all at sea. Dave Watts was fair-haired and chunky, while Hector Payne was a bony skin-head who had been in the prize-fighting game at one time but had lacked the skill to progress far in that profession. Both young men looked up to Bly as a kind of father figure, a veteran law-breaker who knew all the tricks of the trade. They did exactly what he told them to do and never questioned his authority.

Crane was something of an odd man out in this set-up. He was a specialist. He never went into the places that were being robbed, never wore a stocking mask or handled a lethal weapon such as a pistol or a sawn-off shotgun. He just drove the car that whisked the other three away from the scene of the crime. The fact was that he felt a certain contempt for Hector and Dave. They were so brainless. He was not sure they were even literate. If they ever read anything it would probably be the *Sun* or the *News of the World*.

For Bly he had a certain grudging respect, as from one professional to another. He did not much like the man, but did not dislike him either. He just hoped that Bly would make no disastrous blunder before the time came for him to hand in his resignation; but he was enough of a realist to know that the odds were against the kind of business they were engaged in going on very long without something going awry. His desire was that he would not still be around when it did.

Unknown to the others, he was putting money away in the hope that one day he would have enough capital to start up in some legitimate business such as a small garage where he could be his own boss. There was a certain irony in the fact that he had opened a deposit account in a bank for this purpose under an assumed name.

He was living at this time with a woman named Sylvia Adams. She was older than he was; by how much he never knew, because she never volunteered the information and he would not have had the nerve to ask her. He did not pretend to himself that he was in love with her; not in the way he imagined he had been with Vera Gray; but she certainly attracted him. She was voluptuous; that was the word that came into his mind to describe her. She was a long-haired blonde, big-breasted and with a good body and nice legs. She was not what one would have called pretty; not as Vera had been, but she was easy to look at. Her voice was husky, which gave it an oddly sexy character but was probably just the effect of smoking too many cigarettes.

'You'll kill yourself with those things, you

know,' Crane once told her. 'They'll rot your lungs.'

She was unimpressed. 'So what? Nobody lives for ever, so what do a few years more or less matter? And besides, who wants to grow old? Not me, that's for sure. My God, Paul darling, have you seen what old people look like?'

She had a half-decent little flat in Wanstead and worked in a betting shop. From the outset he had made no secret of what he did for a living, because he did not want to start a relationship with her under false pretences. That way he gave her the option of accepting him as he was or saying no go.

He need have had no doubts on that score. She was thoroughly amoral and seemed to get a kick out of consorting with a law-breaker. So much was she taken with the idea that she persuaded Crane to introduce her to the rest of the gang, and there came a time when they would meet in her flat to plan the next operation. She would provide refreshment, and after the business of the evening had been hammered out they would all sit down to a game of cards. She was a pretty sharp poker player and usually managed to take the lion's share of the winnings. Crane had a suspicion that she cheated, but he could not detect how she did it. Maybe it was something she had learnt in the betting shop.

★　★　★

This phase of his life lasted for about a year; but towards the end of it relations between him and Sylvia had almost hit rock bottom. They had been turning sour for quite some time, and the wonder was that the partnership had remained more or less intact as long as it had.

The fact was that they were not really suited to each other, and after the early infatuation had worn off this became more and more apparent as the weeks and months passed. To Crane it became evident all too soon that he was living with a slovenly bitch, some of whose habits he found merely irritating while others seemed to him downright disgusting. Vera and Kimberley had been no great performers in the housekeeping line, but they would have been way ahead of her. As to her dress, she was smart enough when she went out, but in the flat anything was good enough.

For a time he ignored all this and made no comment; but later he began to criticize, and he soon discovered that it was not in her nature to accept criticism from him or

134

anybody else. She told him this in no uncertain terms and hit back at him with a list of things she found not so fine in him.

'You're no bloody paragon yourself,' she said. 'And let me point out that this is my flat and how I behave in it is up to me to decide. If you don't like it you can sod off out and never come back. I can manage without you.'

He might have done just that if he had had anywhere else to go; but at the moment he had not. Some day it would be different; but he needed more time to make his arrangements. So for the present he stayed on, making his peace with her and accepting things as they were.

But the bickering continued from time to time, and one evening when they had had another bitter argument he decided that enough was enough.

'All right,' he said, 'that's it. I'll leave. I'll clear out and you'll be shot of me for good.'

It seemed to come as a shock to her. Perhaps she had not believed that he would in fact walk out on her and was not nearly so keen on the idea as she had given the impression of being.

'You're not serious.'

'Don't kid yourself,' he said. 'I've never been more so.'

'So where will you go?'

'I don't know yet. But I'll find somewhere. Anyway, that's not your problem.'

'You'll miss having your meetings here.'

'Not a bit of it. After the next job I'm quitting. That lot will see me no more. They'll have to find another wheelman because I've had enough of it.'

'You don't mean that.'

'I surely do. I'll do just the one more job and that'll be my lot.'

'Have you told the others?'

'Not yet. I'm going to leave it till after the next job's done. And I'll be glad if you don't mention it to them either.'

She made no promise on that score. She said: 'They won't like it, will they? You walking out on them.'

'Maybe not. But they'll just have to accept it. Like you'll have to accept my walking out on you.'

She was frowning, and he wondered just what was going on in her mind. He could see that she was in a bad mood and was maybe angry because he had taken her at her word and planned to leave.

Then, in a sudden burst of venom, she said: 'You're a rotten bastard, Paul. After all I've done for you it comes to this. You treat me like dirt. But I suppose it's typical. No bloody gratitude.'

He wondered just what she had done for him that warranted this gratitude he was supposed not to have shown. It had always been a case of give and take between them; and though she had provided the accommodation he had paid fairly generously for his board and lodgings. Taking one thing with another he reckoned they were about all square in their relationship, and if he was pulling out now she could hardly deny that she had goaded him into doing so.

He said nothing. And this silence appeared to add fuel to her anger.

'Beast!' she said. And she took a couple of steps towards him and slapped him on the cheek.

It stung, but he did not retaliate.

'You'll pay for this,' she said. 'You can't treat me like dirt and get away with it. I'll get my own back on you, see if I don't.'

It was not, he reflected, the happiest of notes on which to end an affair.

16

Last Job

She surprised him next evening when Bly and Watts and Payne turned up to discuss plans for the robbing of a bank in the East End. She could not have been more charming. It was as if she had completely banished from her mind all recollection of that bitter set-to she and he had had the previous day.

She was wearing a dress which revealed more of her body than it concealed; and when she brought in the cans of beer and the sandwiches Watts and Payne could not keep their eyes off her. She even lost in the poker game and made a joke of it.

'Must be losing my touch. Or are you boys learning a thing or two?'

'With you to teach us,' Bly said with a heavy attempt at gallantry, 'who wouldn't?'

Crane wondered what was behind it all. Was it an attempt to make him change his mind about leaving? Was she showing him just how sweet she could be and what he would be losing if he went ahead with his plan to walk out on her? Possibly. But it would not work. His mind was made up.

He noticed that she had made no mention that he proposed quitting the gang when this last job had been completed. In that respect she was doing what he had asked her to do. Which might or might not indicate that she hoped to persuade him to change his mind. But it was quite useless of course. The die had been cast and this phase in his career was drawing to its close.

Of where he would go and what he would do when he had left Sylvia and the gang he had only the vaguest of ideas. It ought not to be too difficult to find alternative accommodation; a room in some seedy apartment house such as he had once shared with Charlie Green would serve, if only on a temporary basis. Fortunately, he had that pot of cash stowed away in a bank account which he had opened under an assumed name. It was not as much as he had planned to accumulate before throwing in his hand as a wheelman, and it was certainly not enough to set him up in a business of his own; but it was sufficient to keep him going while he took a look around.

He wondered whether he might manage to get a proper job, possibly in a garage. The idea of going straight after all these years in crime had a certain appeal for him. Maybe he was by instinct essentially an honest man and had only drifted into the criminal way of life by force of circumstance and initially under the influence of Charlie Green. Anyway, it would be worthwhile giving the straight and narrow a try. It would certainly make a change.

★　★　★

Sylvia was still being sweet to him the next morning. Before she left to go to work she gave him a loving kiss and said: 'You can still change your mind, you know. It's not too late. It could be good between us again. We wouldn't have to be at each other's throats all the time. We could make a fresh start; give and take. What do you say?'

She was really pleading with him; he could see that. He would not have expected her to be quite so keen on getting back to the old footing. But maybe she had more true feeling for him than he had ever imagined.

'Please, Paul,' she said. 'It would be just like the old times. You only have to say the word.'

But it was a word he could not bring himself to say. He knew a reconciliation might have been fine for a time if she put her mind to it; but she would never change her habits, and the bickering would start up again sooner or later.

'It's no use, Sylvia,' he said. 'You and I, we've come to the end of the road; can't you see that? It was good while it lasted, but now it's finished and you have to face the fact.'

Her face darkened for a moment, and he thought she might be about to yell at him again, the way she had when he had first told her he was leaving. But she kept control of herself. The frown vanished, and when she spoke it was quite calmly.

'Well, if your mind's really made up that's all there is to it. I just hope you won't live to regret the move; but it's your life and your decision. So if things go terribly wrong there'll only be yourself to blame, won't there?'

And with that she left the flat and closed the door behind her.

* * *

The car was waiting at Harry Bly's scrapyard in Bromley. This was the legitimate business which he used as a front for his more nefarious activities.

Dave Watts and Hector Payne worked for him there when they were not otherwise engaged.

141

The car was a Honda hatchback which Crane had picked up the previous day. He had taken it to the scrapyard where it had disappeared inside a large shed and had its number plates changed.

The others were already there when Crane arrived. They had been having a tot of whisky, which was the usual practice before an operation. Bly said it steadied the nerves. But Crane never joined in the drinking; he maintained that anyone who said he drove better with a drop or two of alcohol inside him was kidding himself. Anyone who needed that sort of aid to his driving had no business being at the wheel of a motor vehicle, and certainly not a getaway car.

'How are you feeling, Paul me boy?' Bly asked.

'Just the same as I always feel,' Crane said. 'What's different today?'

Bly laughed. 'Ah, you're the cool one. They're all the same to you, ain't they?'

Which was not true, of course. This one was different for him at any rate. Because it was to be the last. But they did not know this. Time enough to tell them when it was all over.

He had reconnoitred the area where the bank was situated. He knew where he would be with the Honda; he knew the getaway route and the place where they would abandon the first car and switch to another that would be waiting for them. Oh, it was all worked out like it always was. But never again; not for him. The others would probably carry on at the game, but they would have to find another wheelman because he would be gone. He felt a kind of exhilaration at the thought, because this was another landmark in his life; another change of direction; the start of something new.

He wondered how they would take it when he told them. None too well perhaps. Maybe as badly as Sylvia had taken it, with recriminations and attempts to persuade him to change his mind. It would be no use, a waste of breath. After this he would be gone from them and they would see him no more.

'Right then, lads,' Bly said. 'Time to be moving.'

They carried the gear to the car: the masks, the weapons, the bags for the money. Bly sat in the front with Crane, the other two in the back. There was very little talking; there was a feeling of tension; they were like athletes waiting for the starter's pistol.

Now, Crane was thinking, let it all go smoothly. Let's have no cock-ups this one last time; not right at the end.

It was not the most impressive of banks. It was just a branch in an unfashionable part of town, and it had been there for a long time. It could have done with a face-lift, a bit of refurbishing. But perhaps it was one of those marked down for closure and not deemed worth the cost of a lick of paint.

Crane brought the car to a halt, and the others were already in their masks. They took the guns and the bags and went into the bank at a brisk pace.

And that was when it all went wrong.

It went wrong because the police were there before them. The police were waiting, and some of them were armed too, and they were wearing bullet-proof vests.

Crane did not even get the chance to drive away. Suddenly there were police everywhere; it was like a coppers' jamboree. One of them opened the front door of the Honda and another opened the door on the other side.

'You're nicked,' one of them said.

He sounded quite happy about it.

It was only too apparent that there must have been a tip-off. The police would not have been waiting in force at that particular place at that particular time if someone had not informed them that a raid was to be mounted there and then. And for Crane it was easy to guess who the informant had been. One name sprang immediately into his mind, and the name was Sylvia Adams. She must have put a telephone call through to them only a few minutes after leaving the flat. It would have given them time to marshal their forces and set up the trap.

Clever little Sylvia.

She had never been in on the planning, but she was smart enough to get the gist of things; catching a word here and there. They had never taken any great pains to make sure she heard nothing vital, for the fact was that they had not deemed it necessary. They had trusted her. She was one of them. Why would she give them away?

Well, he knew why even if the others did not. And he could have prevented the catastrophe; he had had it in his power to avert this disaster. Because she had given him that last chance; had done her utmost to persuade him to take it. He had only to say the word and all would have gone smoothly: no waiting coppers, no arrests and money in the bag.

But he had refused to say that word, and this was the consequence: instead of more time spent with her in her flat there would be time in a far less pleasant place where the hours and the weeks and the months and the years would pass very wearily indeed. That was now inevitable.

*   *   *

When it came to the trial things were not made any better for the accused men by the fact that Hector Payne had been crazy enough to shoot a policeman in the arm with his revolver. Fortunately, Bly, who was carrying the sawn-off shotgun, was far too sensible even to think of using it. He was an old enough hand to recognize when the game was up.

But Payne's fit of madness told against them all and probably ensured that they would get longer sentences than might otherwise have been the case.

*   *   *

Crane was not surprised when Sylvia Adams failed to visit him in prison. He would not have expected her to. He doubted whether he would ever see her again. And he was quite sure he did not wish to do so. As she had proved at the last, she really was a bitch; and a vindictive one at that.

17

Piece of Luck

He was quite a few years older when the prison door opened and allowed him once again to walk out a free man. He had not enjoyed the years inside, but he had not expected to. Prisons were not designed as holiday camps for the pleasure of the residents. He was there to be punished for his wrong-doing, and he had to admit the justice of this and bear it with all the stoicism he could muster.

If prison life did nothing more for him, he believed it toughened him, both physically and mentally. He came out a harder man than he had been when he went in; and he came out also with a resolve never to go back inside. As a corollary of this resolve he also decided not to commit any act that might be calculated to have the unfortunate consequence of sending him there. In other words he had made up his mind to go straight.

It was what he had been intending to do once that last job of bank-robbing had been completed; but he had been too late, and the result was that he had lost some of the best years of his life languishing behind bars. That must never be allowed to happen again.

He was aware that many discharged convicts had made similar resolutions in the past and had failed to stick to them. But he had never regarded himself as a dedicated criminal, and there was a great attraction for him in the prospect of thrusting all that behind him and becoming a decent law-abiding citizen. He could do it; he was sure he could. And at least he was not without a certain amount of money. It was in that bank deposit account which he had opened when he was in funds. So he would have enough to live on for a while as he looked around for an opening. Something would turn up.

And something did, quite unexpectedly; something which was to change once more the course of his life and set him on yet another track.

* * *

It occurred late one evening as he was making his way back to the room he had rented in a cheap boarding house in South London. He was walking, because he liked the exercise and the possibility of being mugged had never bothered him.

The fact was that he had never been mugged and had never had an attempt at mugging made on him. Yet on this night he was to come upon a case of this activity actually taking place.

It was in a quiet residential street in quite a good class area where there were cars parked along each side. There was no one about at that moment except himself and two others. One of the others was a rather stout bald-headed man wearing a suit. The other was in jeans and a short leather jacket with blue and white trainers on his feet. He appeared to be younger than the bald-headed man, and he was a stringy individual with a cropped head.

At the time when Crane appeared on the scene this younger man had one arm hooked round the other's neck while his free hand was groping in one of the pockets of the suit. They were standing beside the open front door of a big Bentley saloon, and Crane guessed that the older man had been about to get into the driving seat when he had been attacked from behind by the mugger. He was struggling, but not very effectively, and it was evident that he was about to lose his wallet and anything else of value he had on him.

Crane could have passed by on the other side like the priest and the Levite; but in this instance he did not hesitate to play the Good Samaritan. He went immediately to the aid of the bald-headed man.

And not a moment too soon, for judging by the sounds he was making the man seemed to be in imminent danger of being throttled, and his efforts to free himself were becoming weaker.

Crane came up behind the mugger and without a word gave him a chop to the neck with the edge of his hand. This was one of the tricks he had learnt in prison. For a time he had shared a cell with a man named Harold Whalebelly who was great on the martial arts and only too willing to teach Crane all that he knew. Crane was a ready pupil because he figured that the ability to take care of yourself might stand you in good stead, not only in prison where the neighbours could be a rough lot, but also in the world outside.

So when he chopped the mugger with the edge of his hand it had the desired effect. He released his victim and staggered away from him looking distinctly groggy and a bit weak at the knees.

'Beat it,' Crane said.

The man stared at him but made no move to obey the order. He gave a shake of the head as if to clear his brain; and he must have been quite a tough nut, for he was pretty soon in action again. He put his right hand into a pocket of the leather jacket and hauled out a flick-knife. There was a click and the blade shot out and he came at Crane with it. He made a stab at Crane's throat, but he was not quick enough. Crane swayed to one side and kicked him on the left kneecap. He gave a howl and dropped the knife. Crane picked it up and prodded him with it.

'Now get to hell out of it before you get yourself really hurt.'

The man gave him a venomous look. 'You got my knife, you bastard.'

'So I have,' Crane said. 'If you want it back you'd better come and see me in the morning. Right now I don't think you're to be trusted with it. Now are you going or do I have to let some of your blood out of you?'

He made a gesture with the knife, aiming at the man's eyes. It was enough. He jerked his head back out of range, turned and limped away, muttering to himself and evidently much disappointed with the way things had gone.

Crane tossed the knife away and turned to the bald-headed man. 'You all right?'

He was hanging on to the door of the car as if he was finding some difficulty in standing up, and when he answered his speech was slurred, so that it was difficult to make out what he was saying. Then he seemed to lose his grip on the door and might have fallen if Crane had not moved in quickly to support him. He was close enough then to catch the smell of alcohol on his breath, and he guessed that the unsteadiness was more the result of the liquor he had consumed than the attentions of the mugger.

'Be all right,' he mumbled. 'Jus' a minute. Get in car.'

He tried to climb in, but he was not making a very good job of it. He was down on his hands and knees now, half in and half out of the driving seat.

'You're not thinking of driving, are you?' Crane said.

'Yesh. Why not?'

'Because if you ask me you're not in any fit state to do anything of the kind.'

'Didn' ask you.'

'All right. So you didn't ask me. So I just gave an opinion. Where are you intending to go?'

'Home.'

'Where's that?'

'Shurrey.'

'That's a long way. You'll never make it.'

'Think not?'

'I'm sure of it.'

The man turned a watery eye on him.

'Who in hell are you anyway?'

'Name's Crane. I just stopped a mugger from robbing you. Maybe strangling you too. Remember?'

'Shright. Sho you did. Mush obliged. Help me in, will you?'

'Look,' Crane said. 'How would it be if you let me drive you home?' It was an idea that had just come into his head, and he rather liked it. It was a long time since he had been at the wheel of a car like this one. Years, in fact. It would be good to get the feel of it again. 'You don't want to be stopped by the police, do you? Could mean a lot of trouble.'

The man seemed to think about this, and it must have impressed him even in his fuddled state.

'Maybe right.'

'You bet I'm right. Come on. Let me help you round to the other side.'

It took a bit of time getting the man into the passenger seat and fitting the seat-belt on him, but it was done at last. Crane went round and got in behind the wheel. The key was already in the ignition and the engine started without hesitation.

'You'd better tell me the address,' he said. 'And maybe it would be as well if I knew your name.'

He wormed both pieces of information out

of the man in the end. His name was Arthur Wrightson and he had a house in the Surrey stockbroker belt. Crane was not familiar with the area, but he reckoned he could find it. He doubted whether he was going to get much help from Wrightson, who fell asleep almost as soon as they started.

It was fortunate that Crane had a driving licence, and a perfectly genuine one at that. Oddly enough, he had taken a course of instruction from a driving school at the very time when he was engaged in stealing cars. It was something of a joke really, but he had figured that a pukka licence might come in handy sometime. He had passed the test at the first attempt. No trouble at all.

When he came out of prison he renewed the licence. He had an idea that he might get a job in the driving line, but so far nothing had come up. Until now.

He discovered later that Wrightson had spent the evening at one of the houses in the street where the car had been parked. He had been gambling with some business acquaintances and had lost quite a packet. He had also drunk more than was good for him; and when he left the house and came out into the fresh air he began to lose his grip on things. He had the car door open and was trying not very successfully to get in when the mugger came along and got to work on him.

It was really a great piece of luck for him that Crane had turned up at the critical moment. And as things were to turn out, it was a piece of luck for Crane too.

18

A Job

He found the place at last, but only after he had stopped the car and managed to shake Wrightson into wakefulness. Wrightson seemed to have only a vague memory of what had happened, and Crane had to jog it into some kind of working order.

'You were mugged. I rescued you. I've been driving you home. But I don't know just where your place is, so you'll have to direct me from here on in.'

It was difficult. The man would keep falling asleep again. Crane lowered both front windows and let a breeze of cool air flow through the car; and this helped. Eventually they reached journey's end, but it was well past midnight by then.

Crane was impressed when he saw the house. It was some way back from the road and was approached by way of a gravelled drive with trees and shrubs on each side. Finally this took a wide sweep round an expanse of lawn with a fountain in the centre. The house itself was floodlit, so he had a good view of it and could see that it was the kind of place that would have set you back maybe a couple of million smackers or even more if you wanted to buy it.

'My, oh my!' he said. 'This is some place you have here, Mr Wrightson. It really is.'

Wrightson said nothing. He appeared to have fallen asleep again. Crane left him to it. He got out of the car and walked up to the front door of the house, which was under a pillared portico. He rang the bell, and after a while the door was opened by a woman who was wearing jeans and a white roll-neck jumper with slip-on moccasins on her feet.

She stared at him, and he thought she was going to ask him who in hell he was calling at that hour of the night. But she did not. All she said, with a slight raising of the eyebrows, was one word.

'Yes?'

She was a blonde, and a real stunner. She was maybe thirty-five or so, but she had kept her figure and could still wear jeans and a jumper and look great at something after midnight.

Crane thought it would be advisable to make sure he had come to the right place; so he said: 'Is this where Mr Wrightson lives?'

'It is,' she said. 'But he's not at home right now. Who are you?'

'My name's Crane. Mr Wrightson is in the car. I drove him here from London.'

'Oh God!' she said. 'What happened?'

'He was mugged. But he's all right. He's just gone to sleep again.'

She looked past him then and must have spotted the Bentley on the gravel with Wrightson in it.

'Bloody drunk again, I suppose,' she said.

Crane was surprised. It was not what he would have expected to hear. She probably noticed his reaction and thought it advisable to introduce herself.

'I'm Mrs Wrightson.'

Again Crane was surprised. She must have been a good many years younger than her husband, and he was no Adonis and probably never had been. But of course money could buy a lot of things in this world, including maybe a wife who looked as if she might have stepped straight off the page of a glossy magazine. He also thought it odd that she should have answered the doorbell herself. Surely there would be servants in a house like that. But probably they had gone to bed and she was the only person awake.

'OK, Mr Crane,' she said. 'You'd better get him indoors.'

She did not offer to give him a helping hand, so he went back to the car and managed to wake Wrightson with a bit of shaking.

'Come along now. Time to go indoors. Your wife's waiting for you.'

He failed to catch what Wrightson's answer to that was, but it sounded uncomplimentary. However, he succeeded in getting the man out of the car and on his feet, and a little later he was in the house.

'Well,' the woman said, 'you're in a fine state, I must say. Did you have a good time?' She spoke sarcastically.

Wrightson turned on her with sudden ferocity. 'Shut your damn mouth, you bitch.' The words were slurred but not so much that one could fail to get the gist of them.

She took the attack with icy calmness. 'You'd better go to bed, Arthur. If you can manage to climb the stairs. Maybe tomorrow you'll be in a better temper.'

Crane half expected him to turn on her again, but he did not. He seemed really worn out and after the one outburst, quite spiritless.

Mrs Wrightson spoke to Crane. 'Would you mind helping him? He'll never get up the stairs on his own. I'll show you the way.'

It was a wide, thickly carpeted staircase leading up from the entrance hall, and she went on ahead while Crane almost carried

Wrightson. It was hard work. The man was no lightweight and his legs seemed to be made of jelly. But they reached the landing, and the woman led the way to a bedroom where she and Crane undressed Wrightson and got him into the bed. He was asleep and snoring almost as soon as his head met the pillow.

'Now,' the woman said, 'let's go downstairs. Then you can tell me just what happened.'

★　★　★

In a sumptuously furnished room, seated in an armchair that would comfortably have accommodated two people of his size, he told her briefly. She poured him a glass of whisky and one for herself; and now that he had more time to look at her he saw no reason to amend his initial impression that she was one gorgeous female, and maybe a trifle younger than he had at first imagined. She also seemed to have become less icy, which might have been partly the effect of the drink.

He knew now that her name was Renata, and she was calling him Paul.

'Tell me,' she said. 'Do you make a habit of this sort of thing?'

'What sort of thing?' Crane asked.

'Rushing to the aid of people in distress.'

Crane laughed. 'Not really. This is the first time it's happened, and it could well be the last.'

'So you're not a natural do-gooder?'

'I've never thought of myself as one.'

'Well, thank God for that,' she said.

Later she asked him where he lived, and he told her.

'That's a long way from here,' she said. 'How do you propose to make it back?'

'I hadn't thought of that,' he said.

This was not quite true. It was a problem that had crossed his mind, but he had put it aside. He could hardly ask for the loan of the Bentley, promising to return it the next day. And public transport in the small hours of the morning was something that was best forgotten.

'There's only one thing for it,' Renata said. 'You'll have to stay the night here. What time do you have to get to work in the morning?'

'I don't.'

'What, no job?'

'At present, no.'

'So there'll be no hurry then?'

'None at all.'

★ ★ ★

It was a magnificent bedroom with an en suite bathroom. He supposed there were several more like it in the house; enough to accommodate parties of guests, if the Wrightsons went in for entertaining on a large scale.

He slept well and breakfasted in the kitchen with the staff. There was a butler named Dawkes who did not really look the part, being small and skinny and rather self-effacing. The cook was a plump, jolly woman who was approaching middle age and went by the name of Mrs Jones. The menial work was done by two Filipino maids who smiled a lot and seemed perfectly contented. There was also a gardener who did not live in but took some of his meals in the house.

They were all curious to hear the story of the previous night's adventure, but Crane was not giving much away. He doubted whether Wrightson would want the servants to know just what had happened. If he did, he could tell them himself.

★   ★   ★

Later Crane had a talk with the master of the house in a room that had the appearance of a cross between a library and an office.

162

Wrightson looked like a man who was suffering from a pretty nasty hangover. There was some bruising on his neck, and it was probably stiff and giving him a bit of pain whenever he turned his head.

'I have to thank you for what you did for me last night,' he said. 'I'd have been in bad trouble if you hadn't turned up.'

'Don't give it a thought,' Crane said. 'To tell you the truth I rather enjoyed the experience. And it's a long time since I got the chance to drive a Bentley.'

Wrightson looked at him in some surprise. 'You've driven one before?'

'On occasion. Lots of other makes too.'

'So you know something about cars?'

'I'd say I know a lot about cars,' Crane said.

'But Renata tells me you're out of work.'

'That's so.'

'Anything in view?'

'Not really.'

'H'm. We might do something about that. Would working for me interest you?'

'In what capacity?'

'Chauffeur. Handyman. That sort of thing.'

'But you know nothing about me.'

'I know you maybe saved my life.'

'Oh, I don't think he'd have killed you.'

'I'm not so sure. He was strangling me. I

couldn't breathe. And he had a knife, didn't he?'

'That's true. I had to take it away from him.'

Wrightson gazed hard at Crane, stroking his chin in a ruminative sort of way with the pudgy fingers of his right hand. 'Paul,' he said, 'I think maybe you're one tough character. Am I right?'

Crane said nothing.

'Look,' Wrightson said. 'I'll tell you something. Last night there was a chauffeur who should have been there with the car, but the son-of-a-bitch didn't turn up at the time he was supposed to. Picked up some whore, I'd say. Maybe spent the night with her. Well, he's had it with me. He's out on his ear and the job's yours if you want it. What d'you say?'

'You'd take me on just like that? No references, no CV?'

'Hell, yes. I like the look of you. Why would I be wanting any of that junk? Think about it.'

Crane thought about it.

Then he said: 'There's something you should know about me. It might make a difference.'

'Yes?'

'I've just come out of prison.'

He was watching Wrightson closely to see

how he would react. And the man took it without blinking, without batting an eyelid.

'Is that a fact?'

'Yes, it's a fact.'

'What were you in for?'

'I was wheelman for a gang of bank robbers. Somebody blew the whistle on us. Before that I used to steal cars.'

Wrightson began to laugh. He seemed to have forgotten his hangover and his stiff neck. 'So that's how you came to drive Bentleys?'

'That's it.'

'Oh boy!' Wrightson said. 'If this doesn't beat cockfighting! My, oh my! Bank robbing and car stealing. That's some experience.'

'I thought you ought to know.'

'That was very considerate of you.'

'And now I expect you're going to change your mind about that offer of a job.'

Wrightson shook his head. 'Why should I? To my way of thinking a man who used to drive a getaway car must be a pretty dab hand behind the wheel.'

'You're not afraid I'd run off with the Bentley?'

'I'd say it was unlikely, wouldn't you?'

'As a matter of fact, yes. There's one thing I've decided, and that is I never want to go back inside. Once is enough for me. So if you take me on I'll guarantee the Bentley is safe.'

'There's a Rolls-Royce too,' Wrightson said. 'And my wife's Lotus.'

Crane nodded. 'A nice stable.'

And an expensive one too, he thought. But he had already come to the conclusion that Wrightson was not pushed for cash.

'So you'll take the job?'

'I'd be an idiot not to, wouldn't I?'

19

Stargleam

He had his own quarters: a bed-sitting room over the garage where the cars were housed. There was a well-appointed bathroom included, and it was several cuts above most of the places he had been living in previously; and that took in various cells in one or other of Her Majesty's prisons. All things taken into consideration, he felt that he had landed on his feet as a result of that chance encounter with a mugger and his victim. It was the way things went sometimes: you never knew how the dice would fall.

There had been a little unpleasantness. His predecessor in the job of chauffeur and handyman had turned up and been informed that his services were no longer required; which did not please him at all. He was a big, tough-looking brute named Bassie Flinders, and he came to collect his belongings while Crane was moving in.

'So,' he said, 'you're the bastard what's pinched my job.'

'I didn't pinch it,' Crane said. 'You threw it

away. What did you do last night? Get pissed and forget you had an appointment with the boss? Were you holed up somewhere, sleeping it off?'

The insinuation seemed to anger Flinders even more. He became so incensed that he took a swing at Crane with a haymaker which Crane easily avoided. He responded with a punch to the belly, and it was as if his fist had buried itself in a load of soft flesh. It was enough for the big man; he was not as tough as he looked, and one blow to the flabbiness took all the fight out of him. After that he contented himself with letting fly with a barrage of insults which Crane did not even bother to answer.

Flinders left in a huff and was seen no more.

'You have any trouble with that guy who was in the job before you?' Wrightson asked later.

'Not much,' Crane said. 'He seemed pretty narked at getting the push and he took a swing at me.'

'He did? Land one on you?'

'No. He was too slow. I gave him a poke in the guts and it seemed to discourage him. After that he just swore at me.'

Wrightson laughed. 'Carrying too much flab. Like me, I guess.' He patted his stomach.

'Too much good food and not enough exercise.'

'Difference is you don't go around taking swings at people.'

'That's true. If I want it done I pay some other guy to do it for me.'

Crane wondered whether it ever came to that. But he did not ask.

* * *

It did not take him long to realize what a desirable job he had landed. The pay was good and the work load could hardly have been described as excessive. He serviced the cars, and when Wrightson wanted to be taken anywhere he drove him there either in the Bentley or the Rolls. His employer did not even insist on his wearing a chauffeur's livery. As long as he wore a decent grey suit, a collar and tie and a peaked cap, that was enough.

There were occasional visits to the City of London; the beating heart of the financial world; but much of Wrightson's business appeared to be done at the house in Surrey. Men in dark suits, carrying briefcases, would arrive and be conducted by the butler to the library-cum-office. Refreshments would be taken in to them and later they would leave, but Crane had no idea what took place at these conferences. No doubt business matters were discussed; maybe documents were signed and witnessed. He could only make guesses regarding all this, and these might be far from the mark.

Of how Wrightson made his money he had no idea. Nor did he have any wish to inquire; it was none of his business. His employer talked to him quite a lot; he was an affable sort of man and treated Crane more as a friend than an employee. But he never spoke of financial matters.

One day he said: 'What do you think of my wife, Paul?'

Crane answered warily, rather taken aback by this sudden and completely unexpected question: 'I think she's a very charming woman.'

Wrightson had a fat cigar between his thick, moist lips. He puffed out some smoke and said: 'Charming, huh? Yes, I reckon you could say that.' Then: 'You like to sleep with her?'

Crane said nothing.

Wrightson laughed. 'Sure you would, boy. Anybody would. But you're not going to. Nobody gets to sleep with her but me. She's a tart, but she's my tart. Exclusive rights, see? Hell, she costs enough.' Then he said: 'If you want somebody to sleep with, why not take one of the Filipinos? They'd oblige and be glad to, I shouldn't wonder. Good-looking young guy like you.'

Crane thought it possible, but he was not attracted to the idea. The two maids were not remarkable for their beauty or their figures, and he decided not to make any advances to them. As to Renata, he had a feeling that it might not have been difficult to get into bed with her if Wrightson were out of the way. But that opportunity never occurred, and he was left wondering whether he would have taken advantage of it if it had. Maybe. And again, maybe not; since it would have meant the certain loss of a very good job if Wrightson had ever found out. He was a possessive man; and though Crane had always found him easy-going, he had no doubt that there was another, harder side to his character. You did not make a fortune in the City by being soft in your dealings.

★　★　★

Time passed; and then suddenly out of the blue Wrightson said: 'We're off to the Med next week. You want to come along? No driving. Except maybe if we rent a car now and then for a trip inland.'

It transpired that going to the Med meant

171

joining Wrightson's motor yacht which was waiting for them somewhere on the Riviera. The Wrightsons, Arthur and Renata, with a small party of friends, would fly out in a chartered plane and take a cruise along the coast and around the islands of Greece. Dawkes, the butler, Mrs Jones and the Filipino maids would be left to look after the house.

'We'll be away maybe a couple of months or so,' Wrightson said. 'You'll enjoy it.'

It was of course more of a command than an invitation. Wrightson wanted him with the party even if there were no particular duties to perform. He had a feeling that his employer liked having him around. It was an odd thing, something he could not explain to himself, that everybody seemed to take a liking to him. It had been the same in prison; he made no enemies and he even got on well enough with the screws. Then in this household the butler would talk to him in a friendly way even though he seemed to have no time for anyone else. Mrs Jones took a motherly interest in him and often the Filipino maids would gaze at him with adoration in their eyes.

★   ★   ★

There arose the question of a passport. Crane had never had one, and he was not sure whether his criminal record would debar him from obtaining one now. He mentioned this to Wrightson, who told him not to bother himself about that; he could get one for him without going through any tedious formalities. All that was needed was his photograph and signature. And sure enough the passport was produced, looking as genuine as could be. Crane came to the conclusion that Wrightson had dealings with some odd sorts of people; but he asked no questions.

It was early summer when they joined the yacht. There were two other couples who went with them: Gus and Mary Novers and Harry Maitland and his girlfriend Patricia Watson. Gus and Mary were rather a dull couple, Crane thought, but he understood that Gus was a man who did business with Wrightson. The other two were younger and more spirited. They were friends of Renata.

The yacht was waiting for them at Marseille, and when he saw it Crane was impressed. You surely had to be in the money to own a vessel like that: it gleamed with white paint and polished brass; and of course it had a captain and crew to go with it.

The captain's name was Mantell, and he was there to welcome them aboard. He was a

173

lean, tanned man who, in his white shorts and shirt, his peaked cap and gold braid, looked every inch the part.

The guests were conducted to their quarters by a steward, and Crane discovered that even he had a cabin to himself. It was rather small, but was well-appointed and comfortable. He could have asked for nothing better, since he was after all not a guest but merely an employee. Arthur and Renata Wrightson and the other two couples would of course be in more luxurious quarters. But he did not envy them. This was the first time he had been on board a ship, and he looked forward with eager anticipation to the voyage in the motor yacht *Stargleam*. He was sure it would be one of the most memorable experiences of a life that had already had its moments.

He remembered then a day years ago in Maidenhead when Charlie Green had boasted to Kimberley and Vera that one day he would own a yacht and take them all sailing in the Mediterranean. And now the girls were dead and where in the world was Charlie?

20

The Easy Life

On board the yacht Crane found that he had no particular duties. There were stewards to attend to the needs of the passengers and seamen to man the vessel. He was always at Wrightson's beck and call, but there was little for him to do.

He took his meals in the crew's messroom and was on good terms with everyone. He was very soon something of a favourite with Captain Mantell, who, discovering that he had an interest in the subject, took the trouble to instruct him in the basics of navigation.

'You never know,' Mantell said. 'It might come in handy some day.'

Crane thought this unlikely, but it was an interesting subject and he discovered that he had quite an aptitude for it.

'Maybe I should have been a sailor,' he said.

But he did not tell Mantell what kind of a career he had had before being employed by Wrightson. Nor did he reveal the fact that he had been in prison. Only Wrightson knew about that, and possibly Renata. He did not think the others in the party had been told, though he could not be certain.

The engineer, a Frenchman named Vedrine, showed him the twin diesels that drove the propellers. Vedrine was a sour looking man, normally withdrawn and uncommunicative, but even he seemed to warm to Crane; and the fact that he drove cars for Wrightson and knew quite a lot about internal combustion engines counted in his favour.

So, as the yacht went its way, Crane tasted the pleasures of a seagoing life and acquired at the same time a knowledge of the various skills essential to the orderly running of a ship. Such knowledge, though he did not guess it at the time, was to stand him in good stead in time to come.

★　★　★

While the yacht was at sea the ladies of the party spent a great deal of time lounging on deckchairs; the younger two almost naked. They rubbed sunscreen lotion on their skin and quickly acquired a golden tan. Mary Novers was the odd one out. She had ginger hair and the kind of skin that was freckled and blistered easily; so she kept herself shaded from the sun and seemed always to be reading a novel. She appeared to have little in common with the other two and seldom joined in their conversation.

One day when Crane was doing a steward's job and had brought them some iced drinks Patricia, in his hearing, said to Renata:

'Do tell me where you found this gorgeous man. He's your chauffeur, isn't he?'

Harry Maitland was stretched out on another deckchair nearby and Crane could tell that he was not well pleased to hear the expression, gorgeous man, that his girlfriend had used. A frown of annoyance passed across his face, but he said nothing.

'Oh,' Renata said, 'it's quite a story. Maybe I'll tell you sometime. And then again, maybe I won't.'

Wrightson had at that moment appeared on deck, and Crane wondered whether that was the reason why Renata had added those final words. Could it be that Wrightson had warned her not to mention that episode with the mugger, which was hardly calculated to reveal him in a flattering light? Moreover, the host was not likely to want his guests to be aware of the fact that he had placed an ex-jailbird in their midst. Some people were inclined to be rather sensitive regarding matters of that sort.

★ ★ ★

As the yacht continued on its unhurried way the company went ashore at places along the coast: Cannes, Antibes, Nice, Monte Carlo . . . They were living the easy life of the idle rich, and at Monte Carlo of course they all had to try their luck at the casino.

'You can come along as well, Paul,' Wrightson said. 'That's if you feel like throwing some of your money away.'

'Does it have to be thrown away? Don't some people win?'

'Oh, I suppose so. But in the long run it's always the bank that cashes in. You could win, but the odds are stacked against you, and my bet is you'll lose. Still, it should be fun.'

He could not have been more wrong. Somehow that evening the roulette wheel seemed to be enchanted, and the beneficiary of that enchantment was Paul Crane. He did not win with every spin of the wheel; no one ever did that; but he came away with the equivalent of some twenty thousand pounds when he cashed in his chips. For the latter part of the time the girls had followed his lead and they were in pocket too, but not nearly as much as he was.

'This is certainly your lucky night,' Wrightson said. 'I could use some of that luck.' There was an oddly wistful note in his voice when he said this, which surprised Crane. 'You going to try again tomorrow?'

Crane shook his head. 'No way. This sort of thing doesn't happen twice. You come again and they take it all back from you. They didn't build a palace like this place by losing money to the punters.'

'How about the man who broke the bank?'

'It's just a music hall song, isn't it? Did he ever really exist?'

'I don't know,' Wrightson said. 'I just don't know. But I can see you're a canny operator, Paul. Some people wouldn't be able to resist going back and trying again.'

'They're the losers,' Crane said.

He thought Wrightson looked unhappy. There was a rather sombre expression on his face, as though the words had touched a nerve and set him thinking of something he would rather have dismissed from his mind.

'Aren't we all?' he said. 'Aren't we all in the end?'

* * *

From Monte Carlo they sailed to Ajaccio in Corsica; then by way of the Strait of Bonifacio and across the Tyrrhenian Sea to Naples and round the toe of Italy into the Ionian Sea, heading for the Isles of Greece.

It was there, in this world of Homer and the myths and legends of ancient time, that the tragedy occurred: Arthur Wrightson vanished.

One morning, the bright and shining start to another day with a sea like blue glass, Renata awoke to find that her husband was not in their cabin. She was not at first alarmed; she imagined he had risen early and possibly gone out on deck for a breath of fresh air. It was not until later, when he had still not put in an appearance, that she became uneasy and then rather alarmed. She went to look for him, without success, and then decided to confide her fears to Captain Mantell. The captain took the matter very seriously and immediately ordered a thorough search of the vessel to be made. It did not take long, and when it was completed the distressing fact had to be accepted: Arthur Wrightson was no longer on board.

★　★　★

Amongst the passengers there was consternation. The initial assumption was that, having for some reason or other gone on deck in the watches of the night, he had accidentally fallen overboard. But later, when it was realized that the sea had been dead calm and that there were rails all round the decks to prevent just such an accident, a more sinister explanation of their host's disappearance began to be whispered. Could he deliberately have thrown himself overboard? Had this in fact been a case of suicide? And if so, why? Certainly there had been no note left; but suicides did not always oblige with explanations in this way.

Naturally, this possibility was not mentioned in the presence of the bereaved wife, who was quite distraught, as well she might be, especially when Mr Novers began to let fall some hints regarding Arthur Wrightson's financial affairs.

Novers, it appeared, had been a close friend of Wrightson's for many years, and at one time a business associate; though he had prudently severed all connections of that kind when he suspected that the man was overreaching himself. For some time there had been rumours floating around in the City that Wrightson's affairs might not bear too close inspection. There was talk of the Fraud

Squad taking an interest, and that did not sound at all good.

Wrightson had of course been in touch with London by radio during the voyage, and according to Novers some information had come through the day before his disappearance that had clearly bothered him. It could have been that his financial edifice was tumbling about his ears.

An indication that some of it might have been erected on shaky foundations and even of bluff was the revelation that the yacht *Stargleam* was not, as he had given the impression, in fact owned by him. He had merely chartered it for the Mediterranean cruise; and this could have been by way of a last fling, in the knowledge that he was soon to be in bad trouble.

It was of course the end of the cruise. There would eventually be an inquiry. The affair would be splashed in the papers. Theories would be advanced. Wrightson's character would be put under the microscope and the question would arise: was he a crook or merely a gambler whose luck had finally deserted him?

Of the guests aboard the yacht Mr and Mrs Novers took everything very calmly; but Harry Maitland and Patricia Watson were highly critical of their missing host. They appeared to think that he had done them a personal injury; though what harm he had done to them it was difficult to see. They had enjoyed a fairly long holiday on board a luxury yacht at no expense to themselves, and though it had come to a sudden conclusion they had lost nothing except the prospect of a few more days or weeks of cruising.

It was Renata who was most affected, and she could perhaps have been excused for taking things rather badly. Her future was bleak if all Wrightson's wealth had gone down the drain, but no doubt her lawyer would rescue as much as possible from the wreck.

As to the staff back home at the house in Surrey — the butler, the cook, the gardener and the two Filipino maids — they looked like being out of work, and it might be tough for them. But it was probably only Crane who spared a thought for them; and he himself would of course be losing his employment. It had not lasted long, but it had been good while it did.

He thought about his future, and already a plan had formed in his mind. He had won twenty thousand pounds in Monte Carlo, and added to the capital he already had it ought to be enough to get him started.

In fact, on the whole he felt that he for one had not come too badly out of this affair.

Tomorrow, he thought, to fresh woods and pastures new.

21

Contract

He saw the cottage advertised for rent. It was in a small village on the North Norfolk coast, and he drove there in the secondhand Ford Mondeo he had bought. He liked the place and took it without hesitation. All that remained now was to find a suitable boat, and that did not take long either.

It was a sea-going cabin-cruiser with a Perkins diesel engine. The owner wanted a quick sale. Crane offered cash and believed he had got a bargain. Experience failed to alter that belief and he never regretted the purchase.

His idea was to take holidaymakers for short sea-trips or parties who wanted to do a bit of offshore fishing; and in the last of the summer months he did enough business to pay his expenses and a bit more besides.

When not in use the boat was kept in the small harbour with a few other pleasure craft, and there was about half a mile of winding channel through the salt marshes to the sea. The name of the village was Marshton and it had a population of about three hundred when there were no summer visitors. When these latter departed Crane began to feel the pinch, because most of his custom went with them. He began to wonder then whether he had not been a fool to imagine he could make anything like a decent living from this kind of business, of which he had had no previous experience.

And the answer was that he probably had.

* * *

It was when he was debating with himself on whether or not to cut his losses by selling up and clearing out that a man named Fred Woolley appeared on his doorstep. Woolley was maybe forty years old, and Crane, with his experience of the criminal world, classified him at once as someone it would be wise not to trust with your credit card. He was about five foot eight and thin, and he had a slight stoop which made it seem as if he was leaning towards you in a conspiratorial kind of way. His voice, which was a trifle hoarse, gave the same impression of conspiracy. His face was the colour of a dirty dishcloth and there was a lot of dark stubble on it which might have indicated an attempt to be in the fashion, if he cared two pins about fashion;

which was doubtful.

When Crane opened the door in answer to his knock he said in that hoarse voice of his: 'You Mr Crane? Mr Paul Crane?'

Crane said he was.

'Ah!' the man said. And then he stopped and took a long hard look at Crane, as though sizing him up. After which he said: 'Name's Woolley. Fred Woolley. You don't know me.'

This was hardly news to Crane. He had never seen the man before, and he said so.

'That's true,' Woolley said. 'I ain't seen you neither. But that's all changed now, innit? Mind if I step inside?'

Crane looked past Woolley and could see his car parked in the road. He wondered what the man was selling. He looked hardly smart enough for a double-glazing salesman and he was carrying no briefcase.

'Why do you want to come in?' he asked.

'I got a proposition to make. Could be to your advantage. Money-wise.'

Crane thought this unlikely, but he could not help feeling a certain curiosity concerning the man. So he stood aside and let him in. Woolley took a seat in the living-room and made a brief inspection of it.

'Nice place you have here.'

'Think so?'

'Oh yeah. Cosy, innit?'

'You didn't come here to tell me that.'

Woolley gave a croaking laugh. 'Right in one. So I didn't. All the way from the Smoke an' all. Be a waste of a journey if I didn't have something important to talk over with you.'

Crane was never to know how Woolley had managed to find him. He might have heard something on the underworld grapevine. Crane had rubbed shoulders with a lot of criminals both in and out of prison, and some of them might have known where he had gone and what he was doing. Information got around. There would have been some who knew about his working for Wrightson. There had been plenty in the papers about that business of the man vanishing from a yacht in the Mediterranean and the subsequent collapse of his financial operations. Renata's picture had been on the front pages, looking beautiful and grief-stricken. He wondered how she was doing now, and he had a feeling that she would have landed on her feet. Perhaps some other rich man would marry her.

'So let's have it.'

'You got a boat,' Woolley said. 'You do sea trips with it.'

'That's no secret,' Crane said.

Woolley lit a cigarette and squinted at him through the smoke. 'That boat of yours. You

188

reckon you could take it across to Holland?'

'If the weather was good I don't suppose there'd be any trouble doing it. But why would I want to?'

'You could make a lotta money doing it.'

Crane got the drift of what Woolley was saying.

'You're talking about smuggling? Drugs?'

'Nah,' Woolley said. 'Nothing like that. Human flesh and blood, that's what.'

So it was illegal immigrants. People wanting to make a new life for themselves in Britain and willing to pay a lot of money for the chance of doing so.

'Think about it,' Woolley said.

Crane thought about it. It was against the law of course, but he could certainly use the cash. He had made a resolution never to do anything illegal again; never to take the risk of being sent back to jail. But how much risk would there be in this? Very little surely if it was done the right way. And there would be no need to do more than two or three trips, just to pull in a bit of capital. He could pull out whenever he decided to.

Woolley was looking at him and maybe guessing what was passing in his mind; aware that the proposal had not been turned down out of hand.

'Let's talk details,' Crane said.

Woolley grinned. 'Sure. Let's do that.'

He could not have anticipated it, but he had come just at the right time to sell his proposition to Crane. The influx of cash had practically dried up and the future had begun to look bleak, so the prospect of pulling in a few shekels by whatever means had to have an attractive look about it.

They discussed the mechanics of the operation. Woolley had it all worked out. He had a partner named Makins who would be seeing to things at the receiving end, but he said there would be no need for Crane ever to meet him. There were also contacts in Holland; and there, too, all arrangements would be made without Crane's participation.

'All that's needed from you is to provide the boat. Everything else will be taken care of.'

Up to this point no mention had been made of the sum that would be paid to Crane for his services. Now he brought the subject up.

'It has to be worth my while. I'm not doing this sort of job for peanuts.'

'No one would expect you to,' Woolley said.

'So how much?'

Woolley hesitated. Crane guessed that he was figuring out how little he could offer with any hope of acceptance. Finally he said:

'How about five hundred pounds?'

'Five hundred!' Crane spoke contemptuously. 'You have to be joking.'

'So what would you suggest?'

'It would have to be four figures. Plus expenses. You don't get diesel for nothing. And there's wear and tear on the boat.'

Woolley gave a lopsided grin. 'I think we can leave out that last item. And of course the figure would depend to some extent on the number of bodies that were brought across.'

They argued about it and finally came to an agreement. Crane was to get a minimum fee of one thousand pounds plus one hundred for expenses and a bonus of a further one hundred for each passenger. The money to be paid in cash.

There was of course nothing set down in writing; it was not that kind of undertaking. It was a gentleman's agreement, even if neither of the participants would have laid claim to being a gentleman.

Crane found some whisky and they drank a tot to set the seal on the contract.

22

Dirty Business

Crane's boat, *Seaspray*, lay at anchor off the coast of Holland not far north of Haarlem. The sea was calm and in the cool night air the boat was almost motionless. The crossing from England had been uneventful, and Woolley had made himself useful by taking a turn or two at the helm. Apparently he was not without some experience of handling small craft, and this was useful, since it gave Crane a chance to get some rest.

Along the shore lights were visible, twinkling like so many stars which had fallen to earth from a sky that was full of them. There was scarcely any breeze, and what there was had little chill in it. In fact conditions could hardly have been better for carrying out the operation in which the two men were engaged.

It was rather more than a week since Woolley's call on Crane. He had returned to London, and when all arrangements had been made he had come down again to Crane's cottage where he had left his car at the rear with the Mondeo. The two of them had then walked to the place where the boat was waiting, tanked up with extra fuel for the voyage.

Nobody took any notice of them. Crane had become well known in the village and he was on nodding terms with many of the natives. But he had made no close friends there, merely acquaintances with whom he might pass the time of day. They knew of course that he took people for sea trips in his boat, so it would have been no surprise for them to observe a stranger embarking with him.

'I don't know how you can stick living in a dead-and-alive hole like this,' Woolley said. 'Not after the kinda life you've led.'

'What do you know about the kind of life I've led?' Crane asked.

'Oh, word gets around. People talk. I hear things.'

'You shouldn't believe all you hear.'

'Oh, I don't,' Woolley said. 'But some things, they stick in the mind. They have the ring of truth, if you see what I mean.'

Crane did see. He wondered how much information about him got passed around. There was some he would not have wished to become common knowledge; like that con- nection with a pair of go-go dancers who had been murdered in a basement flat in London. But that had been a long time ago, and maybe nobody had ever known that he and Charlie had been living with them. And as far as he knew the killer had never been found.

★　★　★

It was coming up to two o'clock in the morning and there was a thin slice of moon giving some silvery radiance to the scene. Woolley had come out on deck and was speaking into his mobile phone, presumably to someone on shore. The mobile was a great help in this kind of situation. It was a whole lot better than signals flashed with a torch. And it was secret too.

Woolley put the phone away.

'Everything okay?' Crane said. 'No snags?'

'None. They'll be here any time now.'

★　★　★

They came out in a small motor-launch. There were six of them. They were Chinese. Crane was surprised at that. Woolley had not told him. Not that it made any difference; an illegal immigrant was an illegal immigrant whatever the nationality. And who could blame anyone for wanting to get away from China?

The launch went away immediately they had been put on board, heading back to the shore. Woolley herded the Chinese, who were all men, into the cabin. There seemed to be only one who could speak English, and not very fluently at that. But this was not Crane's problem. He was busy hauling up the anchor and getting *Seaspray* under way.

He was relieved when they had left the lights of Holland far astern and were heading back across the North Sea, which was behaving itself remarkably well for the time of year. It would not always be like that.

The Chinese jabbered away amongst themselves and he supposed they were happy to be on their way. He wondered how they managed to obtain the money required to finance their journey, of which this was just the final lap. But that too was not his concern; all he had to do was convey them across the North Sea and draw his pay. No doubt there were certain arrangements made for them when they got ashore.

★   ★   ★

After a time Woolley came and talked to him. He seemed pleased with the way things had gone so far.

'Like clockwork,' he said. 'Just like bloody clockwork.'

'You didn't tell me we were going to have Chinese passengers,' Crane said.

'Didn't I? Must've slipped my mind. Does it bother you?'

'No. It's all one to me. But how in hell did they get to Holland? All the way from China.'

'There's a pipeline,' Woolley said. Which was not particularly revealing.

'But it must cost the devil of a lot. How do they manage it? They're not rich, are they?'

'Far from it, I'd say. As I heard it they save for years, and relations chip in. The idea is they get one into the country. He makes it with a lot of hard work and maybe business acumen and paves the way for more to come over and join him. They've got ambition, see?'

'And if they're caught it's money down the drain. All gone for nothing.'

'It's the risk they take. It's their choice. Why should we worry?'

It was a crazy business, Crane thought. With all the unemployment there was in the UK, all the homeless living rough, industries going down the drain and workers being paid off; with all the crime and the congestion and

God knew what else besides, why would anyone be willing to hand over his hard-earned savings to a gang of crooks in exchange for an uncertain undertaking to convey them across thousands of miles of the earth's surface and into this promised land? What misleading visions did they have of this end of the line? And what real chance was there of their ever making their fortunes in this other Eden, demi-paradise, this precious stone set in the silver sea? The odds against them must have been terribly long.

And here was he making profit out of their hopes. So did that make him one of the crooks? Maybe it did. He did not feel good about what he was doing; it was a nasty undertaking, no doubt about that. But if he had refused the job Woolley would almost certainly have found someone else who would do it, and take the money. So what difference did it make? None at all.

All the same, when he thought of those half-dozen men crowded into the cabin of *Seaspray* with their pathetic little plastic suitcases and bundles that were all they possessed with which to embark on a new life far from home and family he could not help but feel a twinge of conscience. It was a dirty business he was engaged in, and he could not persuade himself that it was not.

23

Partners

It was around four o'clock in the morning when they neared the English coast. He cut the engine and dropped anchor some distance offshore. The sky was cloudy but there was no rain falling. The sea was calm.

'Couldn't be better,' Woolley said. 'Looks like we're in luck.'

'We haven't got rid of the cargo yet,' Crane said. 'I'll be happier when they're off my hands.'

He could hear the passengers in the cabin. They must have known how near they were to the end of their long journey and they were jabbering away excitedly. It would be a cruel blow to them, Crane thought, if something went wrong for them now.

Woolley had his mobile phone in action again. He was talking to someone on shore; one of the last links in that long chain stretching from England to China. He finished the conversation and put the phone away.

'They're coming now,' he said.

A while later they heard the sound of an engine. Soon after that a shape appeared out of the gloom. It was not until it touched the hull of the cruiser that Crane was able to see that it was an inflatable boat; a fairly large one with an outboard motor. There were two men in it.

One of the men threw a line on board and Crane made it fast to a cleat.

'Everything okay?' the man said. He had a gruff voice but in the faint light that was coming from the larger craft it was difficult to get a clear view of his features.

'Sure,' Woolley said. 'Right as rain.'

'Let's be havin' 'em then. No sense wastin' time.'

Woolley moved to the doorway of the cabin and gave the word. Immediately the Chinese started coming out on deck and were helped one by one over the side and down into the boat, taking their luggage with them. When they were all in Crane cast off the line that was holding it. The outboard came to life and the boat moved away in a wide curve and headed for the invisible shore. In a few moments it too was out of sight.

Woolley heaved a sigh of satisfaction. 'All fine and dandy. In a little while now they'll be on the beach.'

'And then?'

'Then it's out of our hands.'

'But you must know something about the arrangements that have been made. Those poor devils are surely not going to be just dumped there and left to their own devices.'

'Of course not. They'll be conducted to the van.'

'What van?'

'The one that's going to take them to where it is they're going.'

Crane did not ask where that was. He had no wish to know. The only good thing about the business as far as he was concerned was that he had earned seventeen hundred pounds. He could use the money.

★   ★   ★

It was just beginning to grow light when he brought the cruiser back to the quayside from which it had departed a few days earlier. Nobody seemed to be around at that early hour, and they met no one as they walked up to the cottage.

Somewhat reluctantly Crane offered breakfast and Woolley accepted the offer at once.

'I could eat a horse.'

'It's not on the menu,' Crane said. 'But I can give you bacon and egg.'

'I'll settle for that.'

He ate two fried eggs and four rashers of bacon followed by toast and marmalade and washed down with hot coffee.

'Must be the sea air giving me an appetite. We must try it again sometime.'

'I thought that was the plan.'

'Sure. Just my little joke.'

Crane was in no mood for joking. He felt tired and somehow dirty. All he wanted now was to have a bath and go to bed. He was glad Woolley did not prolong his stay after he had eaten. Before leaving he paid Crane his fee in cash, mostly fifty-pound notes.

'I hope these are genuine,' Crane said.

Woolley pretended to be insulted. 'Now would I try to swindle you? We're partners, right?'

Crane abstained from saying it was right. Woolley was not a man he would have chosen for a partner and he would not have trusted him an inch. But for the present they were business associates. It was in a mucky business, but it was profitable.

He wondered how the Chinese immigrants were getting on. He did not envy them.

*　*　*

They made two more trips before the weather turned bad and they decided to call the operation off for the present. It was not something to attempt in winter, and as it was the third run almost ended in disaster. Waves were breaking on the beach when the immigrants were being ferried ashore and the boat capsized, spilling them into the surf. Fortunately they all managed to scramble up the beach, but some of the luggage was lost.

Crane and Woolley were unable to see what had happened, but they got the information by means of the mobile phone.

'That's it,' Crane said, 'No more trips this year.'

Woolley, though reluctant to call a halt to such a profitable enterprise, had to admit that it was not something to undertake in uncertain weather. Even the crossing of the North Sea in the motorcruiser was likely to be too hazardous.

'It'd be different,' Crane said, 'if we were using a trawler. But we aren't, so it isn't.'

He was not sorry to give up the business, and he was not sure he would even start it again in the spring. It was not something he had enjoyed doing, but the money was useful. On the second trip they had picked up ten Pakistanis and the cabin had been crammed. But it brought him two thousand and one hundred pounds.

He said goodbye to Woolley without

regrets. He would feel no pangs of loss if he never saw him again. He doubted, however, whether the man would be so easy to shake off. He had a feeling that he would turn up again sooner or later.

24

Advance Payment

The winter passed with no further visit from Woolley. Crane did maintenance work on his boat and, occasionally, when the weather relented, he took small parties of hardy enthusiasts out for a day's fishing. He drove into Norwich fairly frequently, and now and then he would take a trip up to London. On the whole he lived frugally; he had money in the bank and no worries. It was, he reflected, not a bad sort of life.

Then he found Penelope and it became infinitely better. For a time.

★   ★   ★

It was spring, and Woolley had turned up again. He wanted to know when they would get started on some more of the illegal immigrant business. Crane put him off. He said it was too early yet; the weather could not be depended on; storms could come up with hardly any warning and he had no wish to be caught in one.

'You want to risk your neck for a few lousy pounds?'

Woolley said they were more than a few, and what was so lousy about a pound sterling anyway?

'Well, it's no go yet. So forget it.'

Woolley departed in something of a huff.

★ ★ ★

When Penny came to live with him he knew that he was certainly not going to start that game again. He could not have kept it a secret from her, and he was pretty sure that she would not have approved. The holiday trade had begun to pick up again and he made her believe that this was what he was living on, though in fact he was still eating into his capital.

She was not with him all the time. She kept in touch with her agent, and occasionally something would be thrown her way and she would run up to London in her Mini. But the jobs were ephemeral and before long she would be back, much to Crane's delight.

In a moment of weakness, or maybe of desperate honesty, he revealed to her the fact that he had been in prison. She was shocked, no doubt about that. She wanted to know how it had come about, and he gave her a carefully expurgated account of what had led up to it. He made no mention of the time when he and Charlie Green had been living with Vera and Kimberley; nor of the murders. And when he spoke of an informer revealing the last proposed bank robbery he did not mention the fact that this informer was a woman and that she had taken this step to spite him for walking out on her.

'So,' Penny said, gazing at him with a slight frown on her beautiful face, 'you used to be a bank robber.'

'No,' Crane said. 'I didn't do any of the robbing. I just drove the getaway car.'

'It amounts to the same thing, doesn't it?'

'Not in my book.'

'That must be a fairly liberal sort of book,' she said. 'And since you came out of prison you've been going straight? Is that what you're telling me?'

'Oh, absolutely.'

Which was the truth only if you ignored the little matter of three voyages across the North Sea to Holland and back.

'Um!' and she said. And then: 'H'm!'

He gazed at her anxiously and wondered just what was passing in her mind. Had he been a complete idiot to make this revelation? And would she now say she could have nothing more to do with him? That an ex-con was not her idea of a perfect partner in life. He waited for the word and it did not come. What she said was:

'Damn you, Paul! Why in hell did I have to fall in love with you when there were so many more acceptable men around? Why did it have to be a damned jailbird?'

'I don't know,' he said. 'I guess that's just the way the cookie crumbles.'

And he was relieved, because her words seemed to indicate that she was going to stick with him, jailbird or no jailbird. But he could see that there was no way he would be doing any more jobs for Fred Woolley. From this point forward he really had to go straight, because if not he would lose her, and he could not bear the thought of that.

And in the end she left him anyway.

★ ★ ★

She found a place for herself in London; a flat that she had to share with no one. Perhaps she had after all put the bite on her father for a substantial handout to keep her going. Or maybe she had picked up some lucrative bit parts in TV advertisements.

He still talked to her now and then on the telephone, unwilling to lose touch, and she was friendly enough if not exactly gushing.

But she volunteered little information, regarding her activities and he was just left guessing.

He wondered whether it was really what she called the squalor of the cold flint cottage that had been the true reason for her leaving. Could it be that she had simply tired of him and was now involved with someone else? She had never given any hint of this, so he could not tell. All he knew was that he was still in love with her and longed to have her back with him.

This was the state of things when Joe Skene and Sam West walked into his life and made him an offer he could not refuse.

★   ★   ★

When they came again they were in the same black MercedesBenz, but this time they were not in suits; they were wearing the kind of gear that was more fitting for a sea voyage in a small boat: jeans, polo-neck sweaters, leather jackets, trainers. Crane found them no more attractive in this attire. He still thought the description plug-ugly was just right for them.

They took the car round to the rear of the cottage and parked it alongside his Mondeo, which looked like a poor relation in comparison. Then they came indoors to make the final preparations for embarkation.

'All set then?' Skene asked. 'Good and ready for the off?'

'Will be when you've handed over the four thousand smackers starting money.'

'You don't think it can wait till we're on the boat?'

'I'd rather have it now.'

Skene glanced at West with a pained expression, shaking his head. 'He still doesn't trust us, Sammy. What a doubting Thomas the guy is.'

'Oh, for Pete's sake,' West said impatiently. 'Give him the cash and let's be on our way.'

'OK, OK,' Skene said. 'No skin off my nose.'

He had brought a leather briefcase with him, and now he opened it and took out an unsealed buff envelope which had a fat look about it. This he handed to Crane.

'You want to count it?'

'You bet I do,' Crane said.

Skene turned again to West. 'What'd I say? No trust.'

West said nothing; he just shrugged.

Crane opened the envelope and took out a wad of new fifty-pound notes. He counted them. There were eighty.

'All correct?' Skene asked.

'Just.'

'What more did you expect? A bonus?'

'From you? Some hope.'

'What are you going to do with it?' Skene asked. 'You got a safe?'

'In a place like this! Not likely. I'll take it with me.'

He was wearing a gaberdine anorak with zip-fasteners on the pockets. He stowed the wad of banknotes in one of the pockets and zipped it up. The money made quite a bulge but it did not bother him; he would have been happy with any number of bulges of that sort.

'Now can we go?' West said.

'Sure, sure. Let's do that.'

25

Sidorov

Crane locked the cottage door behind them and left the key, which was an old-fashioned iron one, under the soil in a large clay flowerpot which had a hydrangea growing in it.

'You always do that?' Skene asked.

'That's right. You think I want to carry a key that size around with me?'

'But anyone could find it there and walk in.'

'So what? Ther's nothing worth stealing. Who would bother?'

'Well,' Skene said, 'I can see why you're taking the money with you.'

★ ★ ★

They walked down to the harbour. There were several people around and some of them gave Crane a word of greeting. They probably imagined Skene and West were going for a trip in his boat, though they had no fishing gear with them. All the luggage they were carrying was Skene's briefcase.

The sky was overcast, but although the air had a damp feel to it there was no rain. What little breeze there was had a nip in it, and once out to sea there was a bit of a swell that caused the boat to roll a little. It was nothing to worry about, but it was too much for Sam West; he was soon feeling pretty sick and had to go and lie down on a settee in the cabin.

Skene, standing beside Crane, gave a laugh. 'Sam's got a queasy stomach.'

'And you haven't?'

'Nah. Mine's cast iron.'

'Lucky you.'

'Where'd you learn to handle a boat?'

'In the Med. I was on board a luxury yacht. There were motor lifeboats which were used to ferry passengers ashore and all that.'

'You mean you were one of the crew?'

'Not really. But I lent a hand at most of the jobs. Had quite a time of it. Yes, quite a time, all things considered.'

'Looks like you've been around,' Skene said.

'Yes, I've been around.'

★　★　★

They came to the rendezvous early in the night and dropped anchor. Crane took the opportunity to snatch a few hours of sleep before the passenger was due to come aboard. It was a different part of the Dutch coast from that where the illegal immigrants had been picked up, but it was the same routine. This time it was Skene who was using the mobile phone.

West had been sick and was still feeling pretty much under the weather. He had eaten little but he had taken some sickness pills and they appeared to have given him some relief. He was in a bad mood, but that seemed to be fairly normal with him.

Skene roused Crane to tell him that the passenger was on his way. It was still pitch dark, but *Seaspray* was showing a riding-light to guide the launch that was approaching from the shore, and soon they heard the sound of its engine.

The passenger who came on board was so muffled up it was difficult to see his face in the gloom. He appeared to be a heavily built man, though rather short, and when he stepped down into the cockpit two suitcases were passed up to him. Immediately that had been done the launch was away, heading back to the shore. During the whole of this transaction not a word had been spoken.

Skene conducted the man into the cabin, taking one of the suitcases, and Crane was left to get the cruiser under way. It was some time later when Skene joined him.

'You see that guy?' Skene asked.

'I saw him,' Crane said. 'But I didn't get a good look at his face. Not enough light.'

'You didn't miss much. He's no beauty.'

'Does he have a name?'

'Sure he does. It's Boris Sidorov.'

'That sounds like a Russian moniker.'

'For a very good reason. He is a Russki. Does it bother you?'

'Why should it? I've had Chinese and Pakistanis on board. It's all one to me. I just do the transporting.'

Skene laughed. 'You're a cool customer, Paul. Nothing excites you, does it?'

'Wrong,' Crane said. 'Plenty of things do. But carrying a Russian from one side of the North Sea to the other is not one of them. To me it's just another job of work.'

Skene went away soon after that and left Crane to his own devices.

★　★　★

Dawn came reluctantly, it seemed. The sky was heavily overcast, but there was little wind and the sea was calmer than it had been on the outward voyage. A little later he became aware that another person had joined him. It

214

was the passenger, Boris Sidorov.

'Everything going well, Captain?' he asked.

Crane assured him that everything was. So far.

'You do much this sort of work?'

He had a growling kind of voice, pretty low in the register. Crane could imagine him singing bass in one of those male-voice choirs that seemed to be so popular in Russia. The accent was heavy.

'No, not much. Just now and then.'

Sidorov lapsed into silence, staring straight ahead into the murk. Crane glanced at his face and had to agree with Skene's statement that he was no beauty. There was a cragginess about his features and the skin was leathery; it looked as though it had been exposed to a lot of extreme weather, and there were warts here and there.

'You've come a long way?' Crane asked.

Sidorov grunted. It was probably an affirmative.

After that conversation died, and soon the Russian seemed to come to the conclusion that he had seen enough of a grey sea and a leaden sky and he went back into the cabin.

* * *

The day passed without incident and there was little change in the weather. Skene took a turn or two at the wheel. Apparently he had had some experience in that line just as Fred Woolley had, but he did not say when or where. They had cold meals but plenty of hot coffee. Skene and West had brought some whisky on board and it could have been this that contributed to the trouble which surely came. Crane was the only one who abstained from the bottle. Sidorov might have preferred vodka but he was certainly not averse to a drop of Scotch, or even more than a drop when it was available.

★　★　★

And so the evening came and it was not long before Crane became aware that some kind of argument had started in the cabin. He could not tell what it was about, but he could hear voices raised in anger and soon it became apparent that tempers were rising and things were becoming very heated indeed.

He debated with himself whether or not to go in there to see what it was all about and maybe calm things down. But then he thought, to hell with it; let them thrash it out among themselves. It was not his pigeon.

He realized later that he might have made

216

the wrong decision. It was possible that a soothing voice might have averted the tragedy. But on the other hand things had perhaps already gone too far for any interference on his part to make any difference. He might simply have made even more trouble for himself.

Then, when he had only just decided not to interfere, he heard a cry of pain, followed scarcely a moment later by a succession of gunshots. Then all was silent; and it was this sudden silence that seemed to him more ominous than anything that had preceded it. Now he had to go and investigate. He had no choice.

★ ★ ★

He cut the engine and let the boat drift. He entered the cabin cautiously, and he had no sooner stepped inside than he found himself staring into the muzzle of a self-loading pistol which was being held in the hand of the passenger; none other than Boris Sidorov.

Sidorov was injured; that was immediately apparent. Blood was leaking out of a wound in his side which had almost certainly been made by a knife that was lying nearby with a red stain on the blade. He was wearing a white shirt and his jacket was open; but the shirt was no longer white because the flow from the wound was soaking into it and spreading.

But at least the Russian was alive; which was more than could be said for Skene and West. They had obviously been on the receiving end of the bullets from Sidorov's gun; and though one of them had had time to hand out a nasty wound with the knife it had not been enough to save him.

'Stop right there,' Sidorov said.

Crane stopped right there. The gun in Sidorov's hand might have been empty, for there had been several shots fired; but it would have been foolish to count on this.

'You'd better not shoot me too,' he said. 'I'm the one that handles the boat and you'd be lost without me. Anyway, I'm not going to attack you. I don't know what all this business has been about, but it has nothing to do with me.'

Sidorov appeared to see the logic in this and he lowered the pistol. He was sitting on one of the settees and the other two men were lying in the kind of grotesque crumpled shapes in which sudden and violent death tends to leave the victims.

'I suppose they are dead,' Crane said.

Sidorov gave a twisted smile. 'What do you think?' He seemed to be in no little pain himself, and Crane wondered how far the knife had gone in and whether it had touched a lung or some other vital part of the man.

Now that the gun was no longer pointing at him he moved further into the cabin and took a closer look at the shot men. They were certainly dead; it was hardly necessary to feel their pulses. But he did so nevertheless.

And now it occurred to him what a devil of a situation he was in. He could not take the boat into harbour with a couple of men, dead from gunshot wounds, lying in the cabin. Besides which, there was the problem of Boris Sidorov, bleeding away like a stuck pig and maybe also booked for the long farewell.

'Now here's a nice mess,' he said. 'You and your pals have certainly put me on the spot, you bastard. You know that, don't you? How in hell do you think I'm going to get out of this one? Or don't you bloody well care?'

And he could see that this was a pretty stupid question, because in the condition he was now in, with blood leaking from him at a rate of knots the last thing this damned Russian was going to bother about was the well-being of one, Paul Crane.

Sidorov just stared back at him and said nothing.

26

Fog

He thought about simply leaving Sidorov to bleed to death. It might not take long by the look of things. But then he had second thoughts and he helped the man to lie down on the settee instead of just sitting on it. He found a towel and made a pad with it to check the flow of blood, but he doubted whether any of this would be of much use, because Sidorov appeared to be having difficulty with his breathing and he certainly looked like a goner.

Half an hour later the Russian gave up his hold on life and Crane found himself with three dead bodies on his hands. Whichever way you looked at it there was no escaping the conclusion that he now had a serious problem. One thing was certain: he could not take the cruiser back to its normal berth and try to explain just how he came to have three very bloody corpses in the cabin. He had to get rid of them; and the only way to to do that was to heave them overboard.

Before he set about this task, however, he

took a look inside Skene's briefcase and found that, apart from a few papers of no interest to him, it was empty: no sixteen thousand pounds, no money at all. So those two lovely characters had been planning to cheat him. After he had carried out the job he was engaged to do, all he would have got for his pains would have been the four grand advance, nothing more.

'Damn them!' he muttered. 'Damn the swindling bastards!'

But they had already been damned. Somehow they had had an argument with the Russian and it had turned out to be a fatal one for all of them.

Crane turned his attention now to the suitcases that Sidorov had brought on board. One of them contained nothing more interesting than some spare clothes and toilet gear. The other, which was larger, was locked.

He found the key in a pocket in Sidorov's jacket, and when he opened the suitcase he saw why it had been locked. Inside were a number of polythene bags containing a white powder; and it was not difficult to guess that this was not flour or icing sugar.

'My, my, my!' Crane murmured. And for a while he could do nothing but gaze at the stuff.

So Sidorov had been a courier bringing a

consignment of heroin for the British market, and Skene and West had been the boys who would arrange his clandestine passage across the North Sea. That was how it had been planned. But then it had all gone wrong.

Crane stared at the polythene bags and tried to guess what they were worth on the street. A million at least; maybe more. And it dawned on him then that this little lot was all his. And after that he began to wonder just how he could turn it into lots of nice big wads of spending money.

★　★　★

Hauling the bodies out of the cabin and tipping them over the side was not too hard a task, and he managed to do it without getting any of the blood on his clothes. There was some on his hands, but that would wash off, and a bit of scrubbing would remove most of the stains from the cabin.

Skene's briefcase and the suitcase with the clothes in it also went overboard, as well as the knife that had killed Sidorov and the Russian's pistol. After which Crane got the boat going again.

Now, as if to add to his problems, a fog that had been coming up earlier had thickened so much that it was impossible to see more than a few feet into this all-enveloping blanket. Its dampness was everywhere, and if there were any stars shining above it they were invisible now.

Crane steered by compass and hoped that by morning the fog would be gone. But long before morning another incident occurred. He was feeling dog-tired and almost asleep on his feet when it happened, and he had heard no fog-horn to give him warning. The first he heard was the swish of water which was made by the bow wave of a ship. It rocked the boat, and then something that seemed like a high steel wall struck it a glancing blow and thrust it aside and was gone, swallowed up by the murk.

To Crane it was obvious what had happened. The wall had been the hull of the ship that had caused the bow wave. It might have been a bulk carrier and he caught the churning sound of the propeller as it went past. Had the boat been directly in the path of the ship it might well have been sliced in half by the bows of the vessel, and it was possible that no one on board the ship had even noticed it. As it was; some water had slopped over into *Seaspray's* cockpit and the boat rocked violently before returning to an even keel. What damage, if any, had been done it was not possible for the moment to estimate, but the boat was still forging ahead and perhaps all was well. He could only hope so.

That this hope was vain became apparent later. Water had been leaking in for some time before Crane became aware of the situation, and by then there was little he could do about it. No amount of pumping or bailing would save the cruiser. He had to resign himself to the fact that it would inevitably sink.

By his reckoning he was now some thirty miles from the English coast and he thought he might possibly make it, though it would certainly be touch and go. Three hours later he was quite sure that he would not.

Fortunately, he was not without a last resort. There was on board a rubber dinghy with a small outboard motor. It was his personal lifeboat, and before the cruiser gave up the final struggle to remain afloat he was already moving away in the dinghy and taking the suitcase containing the heroin with him.

★   ★   ★

There was still only the grey light of dawn, made more murky by the lingering fog, when he came to a shingly beach and stepped ashore, wading the last few yards through small breakers and carrying the suitcase with him.

He left the dinghy where it was. Some beachcomber might pick it up and think himself in luck, or it might drift out to sea with the tide. He was not bothered. He had no more use for it.

The beach rose fairly steeply and at the top was a line of beach huts. Beyond them a narrow winding dirt road led to a village. He knew now where he was. By good fortune he had come ashore no more than eight miles from his own cottage. He decided to walk there, and it took him somewhat more than a couple of hours, carrying the suitcase which seemed to become heavier and heavier as he progressed. Some cars overtook him, but no one stopped to offer him a lift; people were wary of doing that these days when you could get mugged by a hitchhiker you had picked up. He was not sorry; he would have refused anyway; he was not in the mood to talk to anyone and they might have been curious regarding a man on the road at that hour carrying a large suitcase and with wet shoes and a bit of sea-foam clinging to the bottoms of his trousers.

He met no one when he came to the village of Marshton, and he walked up to the cottage and rooted the door key out of the flower-pot.

No one had touched it and he unlocked the door and went inside, thankful to put the suitcase down after carrying it so far. It had begun to feel like a ton weight. He was fagged out and he felt dirty and hungry, but it was good to be home.

He had a bath and a bite to eat and three cups of coffee and went to bed and was asleep in seconds. It had been a long hard night.

★   ★   ★

The fog had gone when he awoke and the sun was shining. He looked at his watch and saw that it was two o'clock in the afternoon. He got up at once because he had things to do. He put on some clean clothes and took a hurried snack and went outside and locked the door behind him. And this time he took the key with him, because now there really was something of value in the cottage; something of very great value.

He went round to the back where Skene's Mercedes-Benz was parked and reflected that the man himself would never be driving it again. Well, that was the way it went: some you won, some you lost. And Skene and West and Sidorov had all lost this one.

There was no ignition key in the car, but to

a man who had once stolen such vehicles for a living this was no problem. He got the car started and backed it out onto the road. It was a nice car to drive and he quite enjoyed the journey to Norwich. He left it in a car-park there and caught a bus for most of the way home before walking the last half mile or so. If anybody in the village were to ask him where his boat was he had a story ready: he had sold it to a foreigner. But he doubted whether anyone would ask.

He felt that his days of seafaring were now in the past and yet another new phase of his life was just beginning. What could you not do with a million pounds?

27

Expectation

He stayed in the cottage only a few minutes, and when he came out again he was carrying the suitcase containing the heroin and an overnight bag, both of which he stowed in the boot of the Mondeo and locked it. There was not quite as much heroin in the suitcase as there had been. In his pocket was a small polythene bag with a tablespoonful of the drug inside it. It was by way of a sample.

By early evening he was in London.

*   *   *

He had never been to Penny's new abode, but he had the address and he just hoped to God there was no man living there with her. She had never made any mention of one when he had spoken to her on the telephone, but perhaps it was the kind of thing she would hesitate to mention. Well, if there was he would just have to alter his plans, that was all there was to it. But he could not disguise from himself the fact that it would be a bitter disappointment. Because he was still in love with her and he hoped she was with him. And now he had something to offer. From here on in he would not be living from hand to mouth; he would be a man of substance and would be able to support her financially while she tried to make a go of it on the stage.

The future for both of them surely now was bright.

★ ★ ★

It was a flat on the first floor of an oldish house in Willesden, possibly twenties or thirties vintage. It was in a quiet street where the houses were all more or less of the same design but with differing paintwork. They all had little pillared porches and coloured glass in the front doors and square bay windows. There had once been tiny gardens in front, but these had now become parking spaces for cars. There were two standing in front of the one where Penny lived, so Crane had to leave the Mondeo in the street.

His fear was that she would not be at home, or even worse, that she would be at home with a male companion. Both fears turned out to be groundless: she was there and she was alone.

'Oh,' she said when she opened the door, 'it's you.'

It was not exactly an expression of delight at seeing him, but it was not one of disgust either. It was strictly neutral.

'Yes,' he said, 'it's me. May I come in?'

'What would you do if I said no?'

'I'd have to go away, wouldn't I? But you're not going to say it, are you?'

She made no answer to that. She just stood aside and let him walk in. Then she shut the door and led him into a living-room which was much the kind he would have expected in a house like that: quite large, with a ceiling higher than you found in more modern houses, picture rails with a few pictures hanging from brass hooks, some rather ugly wallpaper, a fireplace no longer in use, rugs on the floor but no fitted carpet, furniture somewhat past its youth. She probably rented the flat ready furnished and paid through the nose for it.

'Nice place you have here,' he said.

'It stinks,' she said. 'But one has to live somewhere.'

'And it's better than the squalor of a seaside cottage, I suppose.'

She had to smile at that. 'Is that what I called it?'

'I seem to remember you did.'

'I must have been feeling depressed at the time. Things not going well. It wasn't so bad really.'

'You could always come back, you know.'

'And live on what? You haven't come into a fortune, I imagine.'

'Well,' he said, 'there you could be a bit wide of the mark.'

She gave him a quick glance. 'Are you telling me you've got something in view?'

'Could have. Tomorrow I'm going to see a man on business and it may lead to something really good.'

'Are you going to tell me what it is?'

'Not yet. I want to surprise you.'

'It will certainly surprise me if you're really going to make it big. I mean you'll never do it with that boat, will you?'

'No,' he said, 'not with the boat. Never with that. It's all in the past now.'

He did not tell her that the boat was gone; that could wait until later. And maybe he never would tell her; because then he would have to reveal a lot of other things, like that business of rolling three dead men over the side. He was not sure how she would have taken that, and he thought it better not to find out.

'I wondered,' he said, 'if I might stay the night here.'

'Oh,' she said, 'you did, did you? And share my bed perhaps?'

'That would be nice.'

'You think so?'

'I know so. I'm still in love with you, you know. Always will be. You're the best thing that ever came into my life. The very best. And the loveliest.'

'So I'm a thing,' she said. But he saw that she was smiling as though she rather liked the idea of being the best in his life and especially the loveliest.

'You're more than that,' he said. 'You're an angel.'

She shook her head. 'Oh no, not that. Never that, I'm afraid.' And then: 'Have you brought any luggage?'

'It's in the car. I didn't bring it up because I wasn't sure I'd be welcome.'

'And now you are?'

'I haven't heard you say no.'

She still did not say it and he moved towards the door, then stopped with his hand on the knob.

'You don't have to go to work or anything?'

She frowned slightly, as though hating to be reminded of something. 'No, I don't. I'm resting again, dammit.'

'Oh, I am sorry,' he said. But he was not being entirely truthful, for he wanted her there and was glad she would not be dashing off to some theatre and returning at a late hour utterly fagged out and ready for nothing but sleep. 'It must be so depressing for you.'

'It is.'

'Anything in view?'

'Nothing concrete. A possibility of something in rep maybe.'

'Would that mean travelling round the provincial theatres?'

'It could. Away from the hub. I'm not keen on it. This is where the action is. But I suppose beggars can't be choosers.'

Again he thought that this was maybe in his favour. If she had nothing attractive going for her she might be all the more willing to overlook the means by which he proposed to make his fortune. He could not be sure that she would. He could but wait and see.

* * *

He went down to the car and unlocked the boot and took out the overnight bag and the suitcase that had once belonged to a man named Boris Sidorov. When he carried them into the flat Penny stared at the suitcase.

'It looks as if you've come prepared for a long stay.'

'No,' Crane said. 'The small bag has all my gear in it.'

'So what's in the suitcase?'

'Business stuff. I'll show you in the morning.'

'Why not now?'

'I'd rather leave it till then.'

The truth was that he did not want to risk having an argument with her right then and there. He preferred to wait until the next day when he could marshall all the points in favour of what he proposed doing.

'Very well,' she said. 'But you seem to be making a great mystery of things. Am I to take it that this has something to do with that fortune you're expecting to make?'

'It has everything to do with it,' Crane said.

28

Like That

They breakfasted late, and Crane could not help thinking how pleasantly domestic it seemed. And if all went according to plan there would be many more breakfasts like this in the future. That was really something to look forward to.

Not that Penny ate much: half a grapefruit, a nibble of toast and marmalade and a cup of black coffee. It had something to do with keeping her figure, and he was all in favour of that. He loved the look of her just the way she was; especially when her clothes were off.

He had still not revealed what was in the locked suitcase, and wondered whether even now he ought to do so. Could he not get away without showing her the heroin? Would it not be wiser just to rake in the money without telling her precisely how it had been obtained? Perhaps he could keep the secret by cooking up some alternative explanation for his sudden access of wealth.

But he knew it would not work. She would never allow him to get out of the flat without

having opened the suitcase. The postpone-
ment of this revelation had merely served to
add to her curiosity regarding the contents,
and she could hardly wait for him to finish his
breakfast, which was less frugal than hers,
before demanding that he open the bag
without further delay. His half-hearted
suggestion that the mystery should be
maintained until he had brought certain
negotiations to a satisfactory conclusion was
crushed immediately.

'No,' she said. 'You're not going to get away
with it just like that. You said you'd show me
what's in the case this morning and now
you're jolly well going to.'

He saw that she was adamant and that no
argument would move her from her
position. The very fact that he had tried to
go back on his word had simply made her
all the more determined to hold him to his
promise.

He resigned himself to the inevitable. 'Well,
if that's what you really want — '

'It is.'

With some reluctance he fetched the
suitcase from the bedroom, took the key from
his pocket and unlocked it. Then he lifted the
lid and revealed the polythene bags with the
white powder in them.

Her disappointment was obvious. She had

evidently been expecting something far more exciting.

'Is that all?'

'That's all.'

'But what is it?'

He did not answer at once; and his hesitation seemed to give her a hint. Her expression changed and he could almost detect her mind working and the truth hitting her like a sledgehammer.

'My God!' she said, and her eyes widened. 'It's drugs, isn't it? Drugs.'

He thought of denying it but saw immediately that this would be of no use. She would never believe that the bags contained anything else.

'Yes,' he said. 'It's heroin.'

Too late he saw what a fool he had been. He should never have brought the suitcase into the flat; he should have left it in the boot of the car. But would it have been safe there? No one knew better than he that cars parked at night in quiet suburban streets were liable to be broken into or even stolen. He would not have dared to take the risk.

Besides which, he had been so elated by the thought of what riches the heroin would bring in that it had not occurred to him at first that Penny might see the matter in a very different light; that she might be appalled by the very idea of profiting from the sale of such a substance.

She took a step away from the suitcase, as if the very proximity of the drug might contaminate her.

'Where did you get it?' she demanded.

He had an impulse to tell her that he had just found it lying around, but he knew that that would not do. She would have had to be very gullible indeed to swallow a tale like that. And she was not gullible; she was pretty smart really.

'Does it matter?'

'I'd say it matters a great deal.'

'It was chance.'

'Oh, I see. It just fell out of the sky at your feet. Is that it?'

'Now you're being silly.'

'Silly, am I? Well maybe you're right. Silly to believe you might really have had some honest plan for making your fortune, when all the time it was simply a matter of selling a suitcase crammed with bags of dope. Tell me, Paul: how much are you expecting to get for this?'

He shrugged. 'Who knows? A million maybe.'

The mention of the sum appeared to take her aback and her eyes widened more.

'As much as that!'

He could see that the figure had impressed her, and he hoped that such a large amount would bring her round to his way of thinking and she would forget any scruples that she might have had. Most people would think twice about turning down the chance of handling a cool million sterling.

'Maybe more,' he said; putting on the pressure.

But he realized immediately that he had misjudged her. She came back to the attack with a fury he had never expected.

'You bastard! You told me you were going straight. You said you'd put all this sort of thing behind you. Forever, you said. And I believed you. What an idiot I was. Now I see all too clearly that you've done nothing of the sort. You're still a crook at heart and I guess you always will bc. And I let you crawl back into my bed because you hadn't the guts to tell me all about this last night. You must have known I'd never agree to go along with it. What did you take me for? A crook like you?'

'Now wait a minute — '

'No, you wait a minute. How long have you been planning this thing? Weeks, months, a year maybe? Or did it just creep up on you?

So that when it did you forgot all your good resolutions and grabbed it with both hands, illegal or not.'

'It wasn't like that.'

'Oh?' she said. 'So how was it? You tell me. I'd like to hear.'

And he could not tell her; because, whichever way you looked at it, it had been like that.

'I ought to go to the police,' she said. 'I ought to tell them all about this stuff. I'm sure they'd be interested.'

'You wouldn't do that.'

She glared at him. 'Can you give me one good reason why I shouldn't? Just one.'

'You know it would send me back to prison for a long long time. Do you want that?'

'So now you're trading on my feelings for you. Don't you think that's pretty mean?'

'I don't know. I can't be sure of anything any more. I thought — '

'You thought I would jump for joy, I suppose. You judged me by your own low standards. I take that as an insult.'

She had calmed down now. She was no longer speaking in fury. It was more as if in disillusionment; as if she had thought better of him than this and now saw that she had been mistaken. There was even the hint of tears in her eyes; tears of regret perhaps, not anger.

'You'd better go now,' she said. 'You'd better go and take that stuff with you. I never want to see you again.'

29

A Talk With Woolley

Crane had never had any dealings in the illicit drugs line, and although he had come into contact with many criminals in the past he was not acquainted with any who might be in the market for a fairly hefty consignment of heroin. So he had a problem.

He still had every intention of selling this valuable commodity that had so fortuitously fallen into his hands; for he was not without hope that if he returned to Penny with a pocketful of hard cash in place of the white stuff he might yet win her back. She had said she never wanted to see him again, but often things said in the heat of the moment tended to be watered down to a considerable extent after a period of cool consideration. There was truth in the old adage that time was a great healer, and often the healing took place remarkably quickly.

So what if he turned up at her flat with the wherewithal to buy her a far better one in a nicer area? And then suppose he offered to give her a brand new Lotus sports car and maybe even back a play for the West End stage with her in a leading role. Would not all this persuade her to change her mind? He had a feeling that it would.

Meanwhile he still had the problem of how to dispose of the heroin.

He turned it over in his mind and after much thought one name came up: none other than Fred Woolley.

He was not terribly happy with the prospect of going to the man. He had never liked Woolley and had been glad enough to cease working with him; but in matters of business it was often necessary to ignore one's personal feelings in the interests of making a bob or two; or even, as in this case, a great number of bobs.

So Woolley it had to be: a man so steeped in the institutions of the underworld that he was almost bound to know someone, or know of someone, who would be ready and willing to take a suitcase full of heroin off his hands with no questions asked as to where it had come from.

*   *   *

He had never been to Woolley's place, but he had the address. It was, not surprisingly, in East London: Plaistow in fact.

243

He thought of giving Woolley a call on the telephone to warn him that he was coming, but then he decided not to. Let it be a surprise.

It was quite a journey across London, and it was getting on for noon when he reached his destination. He had no idea how much Woolley raked in from his nefarious activities, but his property gave no indication of any great wealth. It was possible of course that he avoided ostentation in order not to draw attention to himself. Living in a mansion in Knightsbridge or Kensington might have attracted the taxman's eyes, or even worse, the eyes of the law.

The house was thirties vintage: semi-detached, two storeys, pebble-dash on the walls and a bay window at the front. There was a garage on the left-hand side, but it was probably being used, as so many were, for anything but the car. Woolley's was parked outside; it was the same not-very-new Renault Clio in which he had in the past driven out to Norfolk; dirty, a dent or two in the body and a hint of rust here and there. No ostentation in the vehicle either. Crane wondered what he put down as his occupation on the self assessment tax form. Financial adviser?

He left his car by the kerb and walked up

to the front door and pressed the bell-push. There was a sound of chimes inside the house and after a while the door opened and a woman looked out at him. She was, he judged, in her mid-forties, maybe getting on for fifty and probably hating it. She had blonde hair, which might not have been its natural colour, and she had a face which perhaps had been quite pretty years ago but which had sagged here and there, as her body had too. She was wearing a flowered cotton dress, a thin gold chain with a cross round her neck and shabby trainers on her feet. There was a sour expression on her face and she stared at Crane with undisguised suspicion.

'Yes?'

'Mrs Woolley?' Crane asked.

'No,' the woman said.

'But Mr Woolley does live here?'

'Yes.'

She seemed to be addicted to mono-syllables, but Crane persevered. She was, he guessed, living with Woolley. Maybe he would have referred to her as his girlfriend, though it was a long time since she had been a girl.

'And is he in?'

The woman abandoned the monosyllabic style and said: 'Who wants to know?'

'My name's Paul Crane. I'd like to have a

word with him if he's available.'

'Wait here,' the woman said. And she shut the door in his face.

He did not have to wait long. Half a minute later the door opened again and Woolley appeared.

'So it's you,' he said. 'What you want?'

'A talk. Some information perhaps.'

'You better come inside then.'

There was a small hallway, stairs running up on the left, a passage on the right. The woman was nowhere to be seen.

'This way,' Woolley said.

They went into a small room at the rear of the house, french windows looking out on to a neglected garden. The room was cluttered and there was dust everywhere. Crane had no doubt that Woolley would have called it his office. There was an old roll-top desk on one side, a waste-paper basket full to the brim, a couple of armchairs with worn upholstery, a threadbare carpet, some prints of racing scenes on the walls, nothing to give the least hint of prosperity.

'You can take a seat,' Woolley said, indicating one of the armchairs. 'I wasn't expecting to see you, and that's the truth.'

Crane could believe that. He could see no reason why Woolley should have been expecting him to call. At their last meeting

Crane had made it plain that he was finished with the illegal immigrant trade. The man had not changed perceptibly: in so short a time it would have been surprising if he had. He still had that unhealthy-looking face with its shading of dark stubble and the rather hoarse voice with its hint of conspiracy.

'You got something to tell me?'

It seemed to Crane an odd question. It was rather as if Woolley thought he was bringing him some piece of information, when in fact of course it was the other way round. He had come to extract not give it.

'Actually,' he said, 'I've come to you for help.'

Woolley looked surprised and a trifle suspicious. 'Help? What sorta help?'

'Maybe the right word would be advice.'

'Go on.'

'Suppose I were to tell you I've got a quantity of a certain kind of merchandise that I want to find a buyer for, but I don't know just where to look, what would you say to that?'

He saw Woolley's head jerk up, and suddenly there was the hint of a gleam in his normally muddy eyes. It was as if Crane's words had touched a nerve.

'This merchandise,' Woolley said softly. 'What colour would it be?'

'White,' Crane said.

'And would it maybe look like a sort of powder, say?'

'It would.'

'And this here white powder, would it be packed in polythene bags?'

'Yes.'

'And these here polythene bags might be stowed in a holdall or a suitcase or some such?'

Crane saw that Woolley was very shrewd. It had taken him no time at all to guess what was being talked about. And he had been spot on. It made Crane feel slightly uneasy, though he could not have said exactly why.

Woolley had been sitting in one of the worn-out armchairs. Now he stood up and went to the roll-top desk. As Crane watched he took a key from his pocket, unlocked a drawer and pulled it out. He reached a hand into the drawer and when it came out Crane could see that there was something in it. This something was small and black and metallic, and when Woolley turned to face him he could see that it was a snub-nosed revolver. He could see also that it was pointing at him.

'You bastard!' Woolley said.

Crane was more than slightly uneasy now; he was downright scared. Because Woolley

248

had thumbed the hammer back on the revolver and it would have taken only a slight pressure on the trigger to send a bullet into some part of his body. At that range it would have been impossible to miss.

'Now hold on a minute,' he said. 'What's all this about? What's eating you, for God's sake?'

And then Woolley really surprised him.

'What happened to Skene and West?' he asked.

'Skene and West! What do you know about them?'

'What do I know about them! What do I know about them! Why, who do you think put them on to you?'

'You?'

'Who else?'

Crane thought about it, and suddenly in a flash of enlightenment it became all so obvious. For who else in the criminal world would have known that he had ever been in that line of business? Who else could have pointed those two unpleasant characters in his direction?

'You're getting the picture now, ain't you?' Woolley said.

And he was. He was getting the picture sure enough and it was not looking so good. Not with that little snub-nosed revolver

249

gripped in Woolley's hand and pointing at him.

'Now look,' he said. 'There's no need for the shooter. I can see that you're more involved in this affair than I had imagined. But there's no call for the bullets to start flying around. That wouldn't help anyone. I can see now we really do have some talking to do.'

Woolley lowered the revolver and eased the hammer forward. After which Crane breathed more easily.

'So what happened?' Woolley asked. 'How come you got the white stuff? Don't tell me you just asked them two boys and they handed it over to you because they liked your face.'

'No,' Crane said, 'I'm not going to tell you that. The fact is they were dead meat before I even knew what was in the suitcase. And that's the truth.'

Woolley looked hard at him. The gun had gone into his pocket, which was reassuring, though it was still close at hand.

'You haven't told me how they came to be dead meat. Did you kill them?'

'Hell, no. I didn't even see them killed. I was at the helm. I heard this rumpus in the cabin and then some shooting. When I went into the cabin there were Skene and West with bullet holes in them and this Russian, Boris Sidorov, bleeding like the devil from a stab wound in the chest. He died soon after.'

'So then you opened the suitcase and took a gander at what was inside. Just out of curiosity.'

'You could say that.'

'So then you heaved the cadavers over the side and made for port as fast as could be.'

'Yes. But I never reached it.'

'What you mean, you never reached it? You're here, ain't you?'

'Of course I am. But there was this fog. Some ship knocked a hole in the boat's side and went on its way. The boat sank.'

'But you're still alive and kicking. You don't look like a drowned rat to me. How come?'

'I got ashore in a rubber dinghy.'

'Well now!' Woolley said. 'There's a story.'

'Don't you believe it?'

'Makes no difference if I believe it or not. Fact remains, you got the H and you're looking for a buyer.'

'That's right.'

'Only one thing wrong with that,' Woolley said.

'What's that?'

'The stuff ain't yours. It's mine.'

30

Plan

Crane stared at Woolley. 'Yours! How do you figure that out?'

Woolley gave a sly grin. 'Easy. I didn't just point them two in your direction. I was in the deal from the start. It was a three-way partnership, see?'

Crane did not believe it. Woolley was not a man whose word he would have trusted in any circumstances. And this sudden revelation that he was an equal partner with Skene and West just did not ring true. Why would they have been willing to hand over a third share of the profits to someone who had merely been an adviser in the early stages? They would not have been so generous. Besides which, as he saw it, they were never going to handle the heroin themselves. Their job, for which no doubt they were being highly paid, was simply to conduct the courier, Sidorov, to whoever was Mr Big in the business. And then it occurred to him that maybe they too had not been playing by the book. Maybe their idea was to kill Boris and take the heroin for themselves; but he had been too big a handful for them. All in all, there seemed to be a lot of trickery going around, and the latest slice was coming from dear old Fred Woolley.

'Well,' he said, 'if you were an equal partner, that still wouldn't make you entitled to the lot.'

'To my way of thinking it would.'

'Now that's a curious way of thinking, I must say,' Crane said.

Woolley was unmoved. 'Don't matter what you say. I'm the one as is in the driving seat.'

Which was true, seeing that he had the gun and Crane was unarmed.

'Look,' Woolley said. 'Why don't you go and fetch the stuff in from your car so's I can take a look at it?'

'I can't do that.'

'Why not?'

'Because it's not in the car,' Crane said. He was afraid that if he admitted the truth that the heroin was in fact locked away in the boot of the Mondeo Woolley might force him at gun-point to give him the key. 'It's back at my cottage.'

'You left it there?'

'All except a small sample which I've got here.' He took the bag from his pocket and handed it to Woolley. 'You can taste it if you like.'

Woolley took the bag and had a look at the powder inside, but he did not taste it.

'Yes,' he said, 'that looks like the genuine article. I'll hang on to this for now!' He went to the desk, put the bag in a drawer and locked it.

Then he said: 'You must be crazy, leaving the rest in that cottage of yours. Suppose somebody broke in and pinched it?'

'Oh, I don't think that's likely.'

'It may not be likely, but it's possible, innit?'

'Well yes, I suppose so.'

'Know what I think?' Woolley said.

'No. Tell me.'

'I think we oughter go down to your place and pick it up. What you say?'

'I suppose you could be right. But hadn't we better first come to an agreement about how we're going to split the profit? I don't mind letting you have a reasonable percentage if you do the marketing.'

Woolley rubbed the stubble on his chin and looked thoughtful. 'Now what,' he said, 'would you call a reasonable percentage? Give us a rough figure.'

'Say ten per cent.'

Woolley gave a contemptuous laugh. 'Ten

per cent! What you take me for? You'll have to do a whole lot better than that, Paul my boy.'

The haggling went on for quite some time, until finally a figure of fifty-fifty was agreed. Woolley appeared to accept it grudgingly, but Crane was certain it was all bluff. He did not trust Woolley and he had a shrewd suspicion of what was passing in the man's head. Once arrived at the cottage, he would have the game in his hands, because he had a gun and Crane had no weapon at all. So in the end his share would not be ten per cent or even fifty; he would grab the lot. And if Crane put up a fight he could get a bullet in the flesh for his pains, and it might prove as fatal as those that had killed Skene and West.

'You drive a hard bargain,' Woolley said. 'But that's the way it goes. We'll both come out of this one hell of a lot better off than them other three guys.'

'There's a saying, isn't there? When thieves fall out honest men thrive.'

Woolley grinned. 'And we're the honest ones, ain't we?'

'Looks like it.'

'Let's be on our way then.'

*　*　*

The woman in the cotton dress came into the hallway as they were leaving. She spoke to Woolley.

'You going out?'

'What's it look like?' Woolley said.

'Where you going?'

'That's none of your business. Gotta see a man about a dog.'

'When'll you be back?'

'No idea. Expect me when you see me.'

The woman seemed about to say more, but thought better of it. She was still standing in the hallway when they left the house.

'We may as well go in your car,' Woolley said.

'I don't think that's a good idea,' Crane objected. 'I'll be staying down there for a while. We can divide the stuff and you can bring your half back here. You'd better let me go first and you can follow in the Renault.'

Woolley hesitated, and Crane guessed that he was turning this suggestion over in his mind and trying to figure out whether there was any catch in it.

'But you want me to market your share, don't you?'

'Sure. But there's no hurry. I'll hang on to mine for a bit and see how yours goes.'

'Well, if that's the way you want it.'

'One other thing before we start. We're

256

going to be pretty hungry before we get to the other end. So I suggest we stop somewhere along the way and have a bite to eat. What do you say?'

'Suits me.'

'Let's go then.'

★ ★ ★

They had a meal in a roadside café between Newmarket and Norwich, and judging by the way Woolley tucked into his food one might have imagined he had been starving for a week. He ate like a hog at the trough and talked with his mouth full.

Facing him across the narrow table, Crane had a feeling of disgust. He realized now, as never before, just how much he detested this man who was most certainly intending to cheat him; to take all for himself and leave nothing for his partner. How could he ever have allowed himself to become allied to such a rogue? And having once broken away from him, how could he have been so foolish as to come to him for help in marketing the heroin? He must have been mad.

But there was no profit in thinking about the past and the false moves he had made. Now he had to think of a way of outwitting the man; to send him away empty-handed in the final showdown. With the odds now so heavily stacked against him, it seemed an insuperable problem. Woolley had all the aces in his hand and maybe more up his sleeve.

He tried to think of any advantages he had over the man, and he could find only one: Woolley was under the impression that the suitcase containing the heroin was in the flint cottage on the North Norfolk coast; while he, Paul Crane, knew that it was in the boot of the Mondeo.

Not that this appeared on the face of it to be much of an advantage.

And then, as he watched Woolley champing his food, it came to him — the plan. It was so simple; he could not imagine why he had not thought of it before. Though the reason of course was that he had been thinking on such widely different lines. Now that it had come to him he could see how beautiful it was in its simplicity. For it would have another virtue besides that of sending Woolley away empty-handed; a virtue that really outweighed even the other. It was indeed this latter that appealed to him most of all.

He was now so taken with the simplicity and the beauty of the plan that he had to smile.

'What you grinning at?' Woolley growled through a mouthful of food.

'Why, I was just thinking how marvellously rich we're going to be, you and I.'

Woolley regarded him with more than a little suspicion. 'You ain't thinking up some way of giving me a poke in the eye, I hope.'

'Now why would I want to do that? How could I do it, even?'

'Ah!' Woolley said. 'That's the question, innit? Just so long's you realize it and don't get up to no monkey tricks, okay. But I'll be watching you. And nobody puts one over on me, so just you remember it.'

'Oh, I will,' Crane said. 'I know how smart you are. Why else would I have come to you for advice?'

'All right then,' Woolley said.

But he still seemed not altogether convinced.

31

To the Wind

They took the ring road at Norwich and headed north through Aylsham, heading for Cromer to bring them on to the coastal road. Crane was still in the lead and he was not driving fast, making it easy for Woolley to keep in touch. It was in the Cromer traffic that he made a move to shake him off; and in the event it proved easy enough.

He came out of Cromer on to the coastal road with Woolley's Renault no longer visible in the mirror, and then he put on speed and headed for Sheringham. He knew that Woolley would have no difficulty in following him; the man had made this journey before on a number of occasions and would simply make his way to the cottage, expecting to find Crane there already. All Crane wanted was a bit of time with no Woolley on his tail.

He passed through Sheringham and came to a place where a hill, overgrown with bracken, rose on the right-hand side of the road. Here he drove the car on to the verge and brought it to a halt.

Acting quickly now, he got out, unlocked the boot and hauled out the suitcase. With this in his hand he began to climb the hill, pushing his way through the bracken, some of which had grown to a considerable height. He was panting and sweating a little when he reached the summit, and from this vantage point he had a view of the sea, glittering in the afternoon sunlight, a sail or two on its surface and a ship far out near the horizon, apparently motionless.

But Crane had not come to admire the view. He unlocked the suitcase and removed one of the polythene bags. Using a small penknife he slit it open and scattered the white powder in the air. There was a brisk wind blowing and it carried away the fine dust like smoke. Crane took another bag and then another from the suitcase, slit them open and scattered the contents, feeling a kind of ecstasy in what he was doing: casting a fortune to the wind.

He had the last bag in his hand when he heard a shout behind him. He turned and saw Woolley toiling up the slope. He was not greatly surprised. Woolley had no doubt spotted the Mondeo at the side of the road, had stopped his own car and had caught sight of Crane at the top of the hill.

At first he might not have realized what

Crane was doing, since he had been unaware that the suitcase was in the boot of the Mondeo. But as he came nearer he could have had no doubt: the heroin that was to have brought him riches was drifting away on the wind.

Crane stopped with the last bag in one hand and the penknife in the other. He looked at Woolley and grinned.

'Welcome,' he said. 'You are just in time for the last rite.'

Woolley made a rush at him, but it was too late. The blade of the penknife slashed the polythene and the powder went with the wind.

'Damn you!' Woolley snarled. 'Have you gone stark staring mad? Have you lost your senses?'

'On the contrary,' Crane said. 'I think I've just found them. You have no idea what a marvellous sensation it is to cast a fortune away like this. I can think of nothing more gratifying. Especially when it gives a swine like you one hell of a poke in the eye.'

'But why?' Woolley said. And he seemed utterly bemused. 'For God's sake, why?'

'Why?' Crane paused to think about it. Then he said: 'Perhaps because when you get to the root of the matter I am essentially an honest man. Or at least a man with certain scruples. I didn't realize it before, but I do now.'

'And that's why you've chucked all this away? My share as well, you bastard; my fifty per cent as well. That's the reason? Because you've had this sudden idea that you're really honest and all that? I don't believe it. There has to be some other reason.'

'No,' Crane said. 'I assure you. None at all.'

And even as he said it he knew it was a lie.

Suddenly Woolley seemed to lose all control. He hauled the revolver from his pocket and pointed it at Crane.

'I'm going to shoot you, you bugger. I'm going to blow your bloody brains out.'

Crane stayed cool. 'No, you're not. You know you're not.'

'So what makes you so bloody sure of that, Mr Wise Guy?'

'Because,' Crane said, 'you never do anything which isn't to your own advantage, and this would cause you one hell of a lot of trouble. Now why don't you look at things calmly? What's the situation? You're not a penny worse off than you were when I walked in on you this morning. Because you really weren't going to get anything from Skene and West, were you? They'd already paid you for putting them on to me, hadn't they? The truth now, Freddie.'

Woolley said nothing. He just scowled.

And then he put the revolver back in his pocket and walked away down the hill, stumbling now and then.

Crane waited a little while, looking at the whiteness on the bracken that was like a light sprinkling of snow. A million pounds! Maybe! But not now! Never a hope of it now even if he wanted to change his mind!

He gathered up the empty bags and put them back in the suitcase. He closed the suitcase, picked it up and followed Woolley down the hill.

The Renault had gone when he reached the bottom. He stowed the suitcase in the boot of the Mondeo and got in behind the wheel.

For a while he sat there, trying to decide what his next move should be. Should he go on to the cottage? There was no great attraction in the idea. And one thing was certain: he had to see Penny. There was something he had to tell her, something important; and it would be better told face to face than on the phone. Yes, infinitely better.

He started the car, turned it in the road and headed back the way he had come.

To London.

Books by James Pattinson
Published by The House of Ulverscroft:

WILD JUSTICE
THE WHEEL OF FORTUNE
ACROSS THE NARROW SEAS
CONTACT MR. DELGADO
LADY FROM ARGENTINA
SOLDIER, SAIL NORTH
THE TELEPHONE MURDERS
SQUEAKY CLEAN
A WIND ON THE HEATH
ONE-WAY TICKET
AWAY WITH MURDER
LAST IN CONVOY
THE ANTWERP APPOINTMENT
THE HONEYMOON CAPER
STEEL
THE DEADLY SHORE
THE MURMANSK ASSIGNMENT
FLIGHT TO THE SEA
DEATH OF A GO-BETWEEN
DANGEROUS ENCHANTMENT
THE PETRONOV PLAN
THE SPOILERS
HOMECOMING
SOME JOB
BAVARIAN SUNSET
THE LIBERATORS
STRIDE

FINAL RUN
THE WILD ONE
DEAD OF WINTER
SPECIAL DELIVERY
SKELETON ISLAND
BUSMAN'S HOLIDAY
A PASSAGE OF ARMS
ON DESPERATE SEAS
THE SPAYDE CONSPIRACY